MURDER in the RED ROOM

Also by Elliott Roosevelt

The President's Man
A First Class Murder
Murder in the Blue Room
Murder in the Rose Garden
Murder in the Oval Office
Murder at the Palace
The White House Pantry Murder
Murder at Hobcaw Barony
The Hyde Park Murder
Murder and the First Lady

Perfect Crimes (ed.)

MURDER in the RED ROOM

Elliott Roosevelt

A THOMAS DUNNE BOOK

St. Martin's Press · New York

ISBN 0-312-07637-1

As always, for Patty

1

"I see one-third of a nation ill-housed, ill-clad, ill-nourished."

That was what the President had said just a week ago, as part of his address to the American people on the occasion of his second inaugural. As she travelled, Mrs. Roosevelt heard that sentence repeated, over and over. To most people it seemed a pledge that now, fresh from his triumphant re-election, the President would commit his enormous prestige as never before to banishing poverty and hunger from America.

To others, though, it obviously meant something different. To a great many people—especially, it seemed, the owners of newspapers—the President's dramatic reference to poor and hungry people was the announcement of an experiment in socialism. Where would Roosevelt try to lead the country now?

She believed she sensed, though, a new optimism. The President's first term had been spent mostly in putting out fires, as you might say—feeding the outright starving, preventing the total and permanent collapse of the economic system. Maybe in his second term he could address the long-range solutions to America's great problems.

She was travelling in the Ohio Valley, as the President's representative, surveying the widespread suffering and damage caused by the worst floods in memory. For the people in the valleys of the Ohio and Mississippi rivers, 1937 would be remembered as the year of the great flood.

"High water," not flood, was what most of them called it. And these floods were different from what most people imagined. The Ohio River had risen gradually, no more than a foot an hour, and people had had time to retreat. It had risen inexorably, however, slowly, slowly submerging fields, then roads and streets, then homes and businesses.

She had travelled by train to Wheeling, West Virginia, then by automobile down the Ohio Valley. The car was an open Packard, and as she was driven through towns the mayors and other local dignitaries sat beside her and joined her in waving at the people.

People shoveling wet, oozy mud from their homes. People carrying out water-soaked furniture. Merchants piling ruined merchandise on the curbs.

In the village of Williamstown, West Virginia, a gray-whiskered man in overalls was led to her car. He was introduced as an expert on floods. She invited him to sit beside her and tell her what he knew. A little surprised, he was reluctant to get in the car, then reluctant to talk; but once started he turned voluble.

"Army Engineers, what work the locks and dams, they claim they know the river. Weather men, they claim they know when they's 'nough rain to raise 'er. What you gotta talk to is river rats. I ain' proud of bein' no river rat. I guess a man'd ruther be somepin' else. But a man like me knows the river, Ma'am. A man like me knows the river."

"Did you anticipate this bad a flood, Mr. Brookover?" she asked.

"Well, not 'zactly. I mean, you could tell she was comin'. Thaw. Rain. Water comes down outa them mountains up in Pennsylvania. But the biggest flood a man has ever seed? No. Didn't figure on that."

The car climbed the approach to a high bridge over the Ohio River. It passed the toll shack, where the toll keeper first waved, then saluted, and then the car climbed on up, until it was more than a hundred feet above the surface of the brown river below: a river that was still out of its banks and sweeping swiftly downstream, carrying a burden of debris. The Packard weaved on the slippery steel plates that formed tracks over the wooden floor of the bridge. A young man was said to have learned to drive well when he could drive all the way across the Williamstown Bridge on the steel tracks and never let his wheels slip off onto the wood.

In the middle of the bridge the First Lady's car encountered an orange, electric interurban car. The conductor waved and rang his bell.

"How you really know a flood is comin'," said Brookover, "is the smoke in the back yards."

"Oh?"

Mrs. Roosevelt was wearing a black coat with a fox fur around her neck, and a black hat with a sweeping feather. Braden Brookover regarded her with a look that perhaps mixed awe with contempt; it said: a great lady, but also a pampered woman, wearing around her neck what would buy a man . . .

She wanted to know about the smoke. "Y' see," he said, "When folks gits in their heads a flood's comin', they cleans out their basements. What's good, they hauls her upstairs where the water won't reach. What's junk, trash—most of what they've tossed in the basements since the last high water—they sets fire to in the back yard. You see all them fires a-burnin', in the back yards of people what knows the river . . . you can be sure she's comin' up."

"Then the water—"

"She jes' comes up," Brookover interrupted. "Lots of houses, she comes in first through the basement drain, jes' runnin' out on the basement floor. Pretty soon she's a foot deep, then two, and so on. Y' got time to keep ahead of her, but you gotta work lively. Folks carries their first-floor furniture up to the second floor. Then—"

"But what if the water reaches the second floor?"

"This time it did," he said. "Lots of houses. And lots of 'em floated off their foundations and went with the current. I went out with my skiff and saved a couple fellers. One of 'em was okay, his house jes' floatin' down to Kentucky nice as could be, with him settin' on the roof. T'other feller, his house had fetched up on a tree and busted up. I pulled him outa the water."

"Where were their families?" she asked.

"Oh, off to stay with folks live on high ground."

Looking down from the bridge, Mrs. Roosevelt saw what she believed was a piano, floating along the Ohio River.

She understood that what she was seeing was only the aftermath of the great flood. The river was still out of its banks, and it was still high and swift, but it had fallen twenty feet below its flood crest. The debris floating on its wide brown surface was not just tree trunks and limbs; it was everything imaginable: recognizable parts of houses, wrecked boats, whole barns upside down with their MAIL POUCH signs entirely readable, wooden wagons, sodden lumps of wood and fabric that looked like upholstered furniture, tables, chairs, and the bloated bodies of animals.

"Folks moves they goods up to the second stories," Brookover went on. "Then y' sit up there and watch the water comin' up the stairs, one at a time, and y' pray it won't reach th' floor where y've got y' furniture. This time she did reach her, for a lot of folks. Worse 'n that. Lots of houses just floated off they foundations and . . . Well, they floated around this way and that a little bit, and most of 'em got out in the current and–And gone. Gone to N'Awleans, I reckon."

The bridge, oddly enough, made a sharp left turn shortly after it crossed the Ohio shoreline, and the Packard descended a long ramp to the streets of Marietta.

The mayor—an automobile dealer, she had been told—waited to welcome the First Lady to the little city. He and the dignitaries with him wore stylish double-breasted suits but also high rubber boots. From the stop at the end of the bridge, Mrs. Roosevelt could see a town where the streets were still deep in wet mud.

The mayor stood in a foot of the slimy stuff. At first he was reluctant to climb into the Packard with the First Lady. Then he saw that the floor of the back seat was covered with mud, that indeed Mrs. Roosevelt herself wore boots that were brown with it. He smiled wanly and climbed into the car.

On the third floor of the Peoples Bank Building, a young family stood at an office window and watched the First Lady's Packard move slowly up Second Street and into the town's main thoroughfare, Putnam Street. They saw the mayor and the odd, tall, gawky woman known now to the whole country as Eleanor Roosevelt.

"I don't care what anybody says," said Mrs. Harrington. "She came to Marietta when she sure didn't have to."

"Politics," muttered her husband.

"Well, Hoover never came here, no matter what."

Mrs. Harrington stared as the big dark-blue Packard passed beneath the open window where she stood with her younger child in her arms. She raised her baby's tiny hand in hers and waved it at the First Lady.

Mrs. Roosevelt happened to see the gesture and waved and smiled.

Only for an instant. Her attention was focused on the bedraggled people who stood to both sides of the street, on curbs that had been submerged only a few hours ago. Her attention was focused on that and on the high-water marks: conspicuous lines on buildings, showing how high the flood had reached—above the tops of store display windows, so high on the light poles along the streets that it was obvious the traffic lights had almost been submerged.

The sidewalks were heaped with soggy merchandise thrown from stores. Men with big brooms swept mud and water through doors.

Mrs. Roosevelt ordered the Packard stopped at the corner of the intersection of Second and Putnam streets, so she could take a longer look at the ruined stores. Motorcycle cops drew into a circle around the car. People shrank back.

The First Lady opened the door of the car and stepped out into the mud. She walked across the wet and muddy pavement, her boots splashing, toward a group of astonished people.

"Hello. Hello," she said. "I am Mrs. Roosevelt. I've come to see what people need, what your government can perhaps do to help in this awful situation. My husband asked me to come. Whatever you have to tell me, I will report back to him."

The people moved in and began to talk to her. She leaned forward, because she was taller than most of them, and listened.

"Politics . . ." said the young Mrs. Harrington in the bank-building window.

Her husband stared at the First Lady sloshing in the mud. His father had long been county chairman of the Republican Party. In the Harrington household, the Ohioan Warren Harding had been a hero, as had Calvin Coolidge and Herbert Hoover. The Republican Party represented the respectable people of the town.

His little son stood beside him at the window, staring down at the big car and the funny-looking woman everyone made such a fuss over.

"You see, Bill," he said to the little boy. "That's the kind of people that are for Roosevelt. Just look. Sloshing around in the mud. Dirty. Stupid." Self-consciously he adjusted his necktie. "People like us are not for Roosevelt."

"Seems like a good many were, last November," said Mrs. Harrington, and she waved her baby's hand once more at Mrs. Roosevelt.

Little Bill looked up at Mommy with a troubled frown. Why would she wave little Sissy's hand at that terrible Mrs. Roosevelt? Didn't she know that people like us weren't for Roosevelt? People like us took care of our own problems, didn't wait for the government to come and do it for us.

Franklin D. Roosevelt, President of the United States, was in an ebullient mood.

Some people wondered if he was ever in anything but an ebullient mood. That was the image he projected, and some people wondered if it were contrived or if he actually was as buoyant as the persona he projected.

And they would never know. Even the people closest to him, even Mrs. Roosevelt, was never certain whether the buoyant optimism he displayed was really his mood of the moment or something he wanted the world to see from a man who had many good reasons not to be optimistic.

Tonight, dressed in tuxedo, he sat on the dais at a dinner at the Mayflower Hotel, flanked by his Vice President, John Nance Garner, and the great Brooklyn pitcher who was also being honored that evening—Van Lingle Mungo, who in the 1936 season had set a National League record by striking out 283 batters.

"Now, let's see," the President said to Mungo. "Seven in a row. Right?"

Last season, on July 25, Mungo had equalled a long-standing Major League record by striking out seven batters in a row.

Mungo grinned. "Well . . ." he murmured. "It was just Cincinnati."

The President guffawed. "There you have it, Jack," he laughed to Garner. "A modest man. What can we run him for? How about senator from South Carolina?"

John Nance Garner, "Cactus Jack," had a sense of humor that went to heavy cigars and generous shots of bourbon. He smiled. His thought, apparently, was of the two senators from South Carolina and which one would be replaced by this baseball player. The corners of his mouth turned down, as if he took the President's suggestion seriously, and his great, bushy white eyebrows fluttered.

"Problem is," said the President, "he'd have to take a huge cut in salary to become a senator. I don't know just how we'd attract him."

Five hundred men and women watched the President and wondered what he was saying to the Vice President and the baseball player that amused all three of them so much.

Certainly the President had reason to be exuberant. The pundits had given him little chance to win re-election over the bland but popular governor of Kansas, Alf Landon. The *Literary Digest* poll had predicted a Landon victory. Most editorialists had read the temper of the country and concluded that a second term for Franklin D. Roosevelt was just not in the cards. After all, the country was normally Republican. Also, he had invaded Washington with a team of professors and social theorists, some of whom had imposed socialistic theories on the nation's government.

He was, at one and the same time, a wild liberal and a stubborn conservative, an isolationist and an internationalist, a Communist and a Fascist. He hated the elderly, said Dr. Townsend. God was against him, Father Coughlin had screamed into his radio microphones. He was suffering syphilis in its last stages, some had charged. He had been infected with it by his wife, who had gotten it from a Negro, the charge went on. He was a would-be dictator. He lacked the courage to be a dictator. And . . .

He had been elected to a second term as President of the United States by the greatest popular-vote margin in history and the greatest electoral-college vote since 1820.

Franklin D. Roosevelt was entitled to his ebullient mood.

He was where he liked to be: in front of a large audience that was waiting to hear the speech he would make in a little while. He was enjoying an elaborate and delicious dinner, in contrast to his usual tray in bed. He would remain after dinner and the speeches and have another drink or two with friends before he returned to the White House.

Professor Felix Frankfurter walked toward the speakers' table. Secret Service men moved to block his approach to the President, but the President pointed and nodded, and they let the professor pass. He leaned forward over the table and shook hands.

"Mr. President," said the famous professor of law. "I just stepped up to say hello."

"I'm glad you did," said the President. "I'd like to see

you at the office tomorrow, if you can come. I'd like to review something with you."

"I . . . Well, certainly. I wa going back to Boston in the morning, but—"

"We'll make it a morning appointment, and you can catch an afternoon train."

"All right. Fine. Can I have a hint as to what we are going to talk about?"

"Professor, I'm going to do something about the Supreme Court. The infamous Nine Old Men have knocked down too many of our programs. I'm going to introduce a court reform bill. I want to review it with you."

Frankfurter frowned. "Reform the Supreme Court? How?"

"By adding some seats—to which I can appoint more liberal justices."

The frown turned to a scowl. "You'll be skating on thin ice, Mr. President," he said. "They'll call it 'packing' the Court, and you'll have a hard time getting support. I'd think hard on this one."

"That's what I am doing, and that's why I want to talk it over in detail with you, Professor," said the President.

Frankfurter shrugged, then smiled. "I'll report to the White House at nine o'clock, then."

The President grinned and once more shook the professor's hand. "Think I'm heading into a fight, hey? Good. I love a good fight."

2

On Wednesday evening, February 3, the President and Mrs. Roosevelt hosted the annual reception and dinner for the judiciary. It was another of those occasions the President so much enjoyed: a full and formal dinner, with music, the gentlemen in white tie, and the ladies in gowns, long white gloves, and smothered in jewelry.

The President was more ebullient than ever that evening, and even Mrs. Roosevelt did not know why. He was feeling foxy. On Friday morning he would announce his court-packing plan; and here they were—except Stone and Brandeis, who were ill that evening—the Nine Old Men in the wrinkled flesh. As he chatted with the justices, he alone knew the secret.

Actually, one other man also knew—Attorney General Homer Cummings—and the knowledge made him uncomfortable. Unlike the President, he did not look forward to the furor that was about to be unleashed. Unlike the President, he was not amused to be carrying the secret of the impending attack on the Court, while shaking hands and exchanging pleasantries and smiles with the very men who were about to be attacked.

Mrs. Roosevelt was led in to dinner by the stately Chief Justice Charles Evans Hughes: a tall, erect, rigid septuagenarian, with a bald head surrounded by a fringe of white hair, and a great, conscientiously trimmed white beard. Mrs. Roosevelt was as tall as he was, though, and was in her own way stately, too. She wore a white silk dress, white gloves, and simple jewelry. People bowed to them as they entered the State Dining Room and took their places side by side at the President's table.

When the string orchestra had played "Hail to the Chief" and "The Star Spangled Banner," the guests were seated, and the First Lady opened a conversation with the chief justice.

"Mr. Chief Justice," she said, "tell me what you think of the new picture magazine, *Life*."

The magazine had been initiated in November, and about ten issues had now appeared, impressing everyone with the new photojournalism.

"I can tell you what one lady said of it," the chief justice responded. "A house-to-house salesman appeared at her door three times, trying to sell her a subscription to *Life*. Well, her little grandson overheard this, and he asked his grandmother, 'Gran'ma, what's *Life*?' And she answered, 'Life is what I'll have if I buy this young man's subscription—'cause he'll pester me to death if I don't buy it.' "

Mrs. Roosevelt joined the chief justice's quiet laughter.

Charles Evans Hughes had served on the Supreme Court from 1910 to 1916, had resigned to run for President against Woodrow Wilson, and had been again appointed to the Court by Herbert Hoover. A man of awe-inspiring dignity, he was also respected for his powerful intellect. Except for the President himself, Charles Evans Hughes was possibly the most prestigious American alive.

He changed the subject. "I understand you made a tour of inspection in the flood-ravaged areas."

"Indeed," she said.

"There are stories," he said, "to the effect that many people made no effort to carry their furniture out of their homes as the water rose—being confident that the government would buy them new household goods if they just let the water come up and ruin them."

"There are always stories of that kind," she said. "Whenever there is suffering, some people will try to rationalize their lack of humanitarian concern by arguing that the sufferers didn't do, or aren't doing, enough to alleviate their own hardship."

The chief justice's face darkened a little above his white beard. As she knew, his personal instincts were humanitarian, even liberal. His mind and conscience wrestled with problems of constitutional interpretation: whether the Founding Fathers had expected the federal government to take responsibility for a host of social problems and try to solve them. His mind said they had not formed a government that should even consider trying to build a society without human suffering. His conscience insisted otherwise.

For example, the Supreme Court had ruled unconstitutional a New York State "anti-sweatshop" law fixing minimum wages for women in industry—model legislation that had also been adopted by six other states. The chief justice had dissented from the majority opinion, writing "I can find nothing in the Federal Constitution which denies to the state the power to protect women from being exploited by overreaching employers through the refusal of a fair wage . . ." He had not, even so, taken a strong position, one strong enough to win over one or two justices and so save the law. The President, who was infuriated at the decision, knew that Charles Evans Hughes had wrestled with his conscience; but, in the President's view, the chief justice did not come down often enough, or strongly enough, on the liberal side. Hughes would take the President's fire along with the moss-backed. Only Brandeis, Stone, and Cardozo would escape the Rooseveltian wrath.

But tonight neither the chief justice nor Mrs. Roosevelt suspected what was coming on Friday, and they chatted comfortably; two people who could disagree and still respect each other.

Mrs. Roosevelt did not notice—or if she noticed she pretended she did not—that the great majority of the guests left their wine glasses untouched. She had told the housekeeper to use what they usually served, a New York State white wine. It was not only inexpensive, it was American; and the fact that no one drank it saved money. Many of the guests only sniffed it before pushing their glasses disdainfully aside. Some took a sip. For most, one sip was enough. Only the most unsophisticated drank the sweetish stuff—and, in fact, the First Lady herself slowly sipped just one glass during the course of the dinner.

The President was embarrassed. He had specifically ordered French champagne for the judiciary dinner. But the First Lady was chatelaine of the White House and had overruled him. So far as she was concerned, people drank too much anyway. Besides which, the Congress didn't appropriate enough entertainment money for the White House to allow her to serve French champagnes.

As everyone was eating soup, a messenger slipped up beside the First Lady and handed her a note. She smiled at the guests to either side of her and opened it in her lap. It read:

> Do not allow any guest to enter the Red Room. It is guarded, but no one should try to enter. I will explain later. I will be available to meet with you as soon as you have a few minutes.
>
> Szczygiel

Stanlislaw Szczygiel (who, thank God, pronounced his name "Siegal") was a veteran Secret Service agent who had last year officially conducted the investigation into the murder of Vivian Taliafero, whose body had been found in the White House rose garden. Although much too fond of gin, he had proven an expert investigator, had accepted her help in a difficult and complex case, and had done his work so circumspectly that hardly a word of the politically significant case had escaped the precincts of the White House.

She stared thoughtfully at his note for a long moment. Yes—as soon as she had a few minutes.

The President would have liked to chat with Justice Louis Brandeis. Or with Harlan Stone. He felt privileged, though—and he knew his wife had set the table up to make it possible—to have the other liberal member of the Court seated where they could talk. That other member was the white-thatched, beetle-browed Benjamin Cardozo.

The President was a lawyer, but he was sufficiently conscious of his own limitations to know his assessment of a jurist didn't amount to much. Even so, he believed Cardozo would earn and sustain in American law a reputation only a little below that of Oliver Wendell Holmes and Louie Brandeis. He had read Cardozo's opinions. He found in them a commitment to the Constitution, coupled with understanding—the understanding that the Constitution had to be read to make it possible for judges today to cope with problems the dear old Founding Fathers in Philadelphia had never guessed might arise.

The President liked that. He didn't believe, couldn't believe, that a nation with problems to solve had to be rigidly bound inside guidelines set a century-and-a-half before. He believed, putting it simply, that George Washington and Benjamin Franklin, Alexander Hamilton and James Madison, and all the rest of them, wrote the Constitution chiefly to cope with the problems of their time and would be the first men in the world to interpret it broadly to make it possible, within its framework, to cope with the difficulties of today.

"Holmes," he said to Cardozo, "used to go to the burlesque theaters here in Washington and the ones in Boston, and stare at the girls taking off their clothes and showing parts of themselves that society generally says they shouldn't expose. How do you think he would have treated a city ordinance that tells young women they can't dance on the stage in anything less than snow suits?"

Benjamin Cardozo laughed. "Mr. President," he said.

"There is an indisputable constitutional right to appear on the stage in the altogethers, if that's what a girl wants to do. A major constitutional problem! Fine way for some cheap-shot senator to turn our attention away from the *real* problems. If you don't care about people starving, blow your horn about *morals*—whatever those may be. There are votes to be had, in the hookworm belt—"

"*Damn*!" the President interrupted. "'Hookworm belt' you read H. L. Mencken!"

"Every chance I get," Cardozo laughed. "And I retain the right to disagree with ninety per cent of what he says. But what he says . . . should be said."

The President nodded and laughed. "He hates me with a burning passion. If he knew I read his every word, he—"

"No, he wouldn't," laughed Cardozo. "He would not be so flattered that he'd change his opinion."

The President laughed heartily.

This was something more that he liked: witty conversation with people who had enough intellect to thrust and parry and still to laugh.

The time came for the President to speak, then for the chief justice to respond.

A secret service man pulled the President's chair back, then knelt to lock the braces on his legs. With the man's help, Franklin Roosevelt rose to his feet and braced himself with his hands on the table, behind a bank of flowers. Two microphones had been pushed into place, and he smiled at the dinner guests and spoke:

"None of you knew my father. Like all Hudson Valley Dutchmen, he used words in an idiosyncratic way. He was like Humpty Dumpty. When he used a word, it meant what he wanted it to mean.

"For example, there is an English-language word 'larrup.' If you look in a dictionary, it means to whip. You give a bad boy a 'larruping.' Well, my father didn't use the word that way. I never did know exactly what he meant by 'larrup,' but it was obviously some kind of sticky, maybe not-altogether-pleasant fluid. Like sorghum molasses. I can remember him saying at the breakfast table, 'You want some of this larrup?' That was syrup. Or at dinner—'Please pass the larrup,' which meant gravy. And sometimes I think he meant glue.

"Well . . ."

He paused and grinned and lifted his wine glass.

"I can't ask you to toast the learned and distinguished judges here tonight with this larrup. So—"

He put the wine down and lifted his water glass as the dinner guests erupted in loud laughter, then in applause.

"Mr. Chief Justice Hughes—"

That little joke sat ill with the First Lady. Bad jokes from many quarters, that she did not serve fine meals in the White House, had long sat ill with her. She was practiced and skilled, though, in concealing her emotions. Years with Franklin had taught her. She continued to chat with the chief justice and with Mrs. Cummings, wife of the attorney general, who was seated next to her.

The note from Stan Szczygiel had captured a part of her attention, and she was anxious to see what he meant by demanding she keep guests away from the Red Room.

At last the speeches ended. Franklin had spoken. And Chief Justice Hughes. And the attorney general. And

Justice Van Devanter. And the president of the American Bar Association, then the chairmen of the House and Senate Judiciary Committees. People pretended to be interested. She could not imagine anyone really was. The speeches were formal, and nothing special was said.

After the speeches she had to linger for a long time in the State Dining Room, then in the hall, bidding a personal good-bye to half the guests.

At last Franklin was wheeled to the elevator, waving a last farewell to the few people left. It was a signal to them that they should make an efficient departure—which they did.

The Red Room was adjacent to the State Dining Room. It was where the President had presided over a private cocktail party just before dinner. The evening's guests had come in three categories: a very few people—the attorney general, Justice Cardozo, Harry Hopkins, and the like—invited to share a drink with the President in his private quarters on the second floor; a small number of distinguished individuals, including the chief justice, invited to the Red Room just before dinner; and the vast majority of the night's crowd, invited only to the dinner. Anyway, only when the guests went in to dinner had the Red Room been vacated. Why in the world would Stan Szczygiel suggest that she should allow no one to return there?

But it was plain that the Secret Service had closed off the Red Room. An agent, meant to be inconspicuous but certainly not succeeding, guarded the door between the great Cross Hall and the Red Room. As the last guests turned into the Entrance Hall and walked toward the North Portico, Mrs. Roosevelt went to the agent at the door.

"Where is Mr. Szczygiel?" she asked.

"Inside, Ma'am."

"Tell him that I wish to see him."

The man went inside the Red Room, and in a moment Szczygiel came out.

"What is going on, Mr. Szczygiel?" she asked.

"Ma'am," he said. "I am afraid there has been a murder in the Red Room."

That there had indeed been a murder in the Red Room was apparent as soon as she entered.

An ominous shape, covered by a sheet, lay on the floor in front of the fireplace. A gray hat, apparently fallen from the body, lay on the hearth.

"If I may suggest it, Ma'am," said Szczygiel, "you don't want to see him. He's not a pretty corpse."

"Come, Mr. Szczygiel. I have seen corpses before. They are none of them pretty. I am not squeamish. And you will remember that I gave you a bit of help in solving the Taliafero murder."

"Help? You solved it yourself, Ma'am. I helped you, not the other way around."

"Then throw back the sheet, Mr. Szczygiel," she said.

Szczygiel remained reluctant. About sixty years old, he was squat and square, both of face and physique. Perhaps his most memorable feature was his oversized, gin-reddened nose. He was wearing a dark-brown double-breasted suit that made him look all the wider. Mrs. Roosevelt smelled the acrid stench of a cigar in the room and suspected he had thrown it out the window when he knew she was about to enter.

"Mr. Szczygiel . . ." she said, prompting him to uncover the body on the floor.

Szczygiel reached down and pulled away the sheet.

The body on the floor was that of a man roughly Szczygiel's own age. It lay on its back, its white collar and blue, flower-patterned necktie soaked with blood. It was dressed in one of those cream-colored suits currently so fashionable, which had exaggerated wide lapels. The yellowish-white hair had been so firmly plastered down with a scented hair oil that not a stand had been knocked out of place by the man's fall. The slightly pouted lips of his wide mouth suggested resentment at the rude and abrupt termination of his life.

"Has the medical examiner seen him?" asked Mrs. Roosevelt.

"Admiral McIntyre looked him over," said Szczygiel. McIntyre was the official White House physician, a navy doctor assigned to the President. "We felt we couldn't remove him from this room until all tonight's guests are out of the house. Lieutenant Kennelly is on his way. The body will be taken in for autopsy."

Mrs. Roosevelt stared thoughtfully at the bloody corpse. "I guess I need not ask how he died," she said quietly.

"Actually, you do. We turned him over. He was lying on his stomach when he was found. He has six or seven stab wounds in his back."

"Do you have any idea who he is?"

"None."

"And no idea what he was doing in the White House?"

"Not yet. We really couldn't do much investigating so long as the White House was crowded with distinguished visitors. We did increase security around the President—we hope inconspicuously."

Mrs. Roosevelt smiled. "I don't think he's aware of it. He has returned upstairs and is having a nightcap with a few friends. I . . . . I believe I shall not tell him about this tonight. It can wait until we have more information."

The President, actually, was not having "a nightcap with a few friends." He was having a nightcap with one man who was his friend, Harry Hopkins, one who was a political ally, Claude Pepper, and one who had piqued his curiosity, George M. Cohan.

He had already promised Pepper, a congressman from Florida, that he would support him if he chose to run for the Senate next year; and he had invited him to the judiciary dinner tonight as a means of giving Pepper more prominence and of underlining the congressman's close relationship with the President.

Cohan had not been at the dinner. He had been invited specifically for the nightcap. George M. Cohan was starring in a Broadway musical called *I'd Rather Be Right*, in which he played the President. The President had heard that Cohan burlesqued him broadly, with ribald humor. He was curious, but he also wanted Cohan to understand that he felt no ill will.

Everyone had dined, but Hopkins had nevertheless ordered two dozen oysters brought up from the White House kitchen, as was his habit late at night. He washed them down with bourbon. Pepper and Cohan, who had declined the oysters, watched curiously at how joyfully Hopkins relished the strange combination. The President, who could appreciate oysters with a dry martini, ate a couple as he sipped on his single cocktail.

"Mr. Cohan," he said with a sly grin, "I understand you do a marvelous imitation of me."

Cohan, who was a few years older than the President, demonstrated that an Irish singer and dancer who had lived his life on the stage could still blush. "Mr. President," he said. "I—"

"I invited you here this evening to show me a little sample," said the President, his grin staying sly.

"Oh, Mr. President! Really, I couldn't."

"Why not? We're friends here. I know I'll enjoy it. I can't come to New York to see the show, so . . . . Please, Mr. Cohan."

Cohan put aside his drink. He sat erect and drew back his shoulders, and he tipped his chin up. "My friends . . ." he said, tossing his head. "Day before yester-*day* . . . Feb-rary *first*, nineteen hundred thirty-seven—" He lowered his head, shook his jowls a little, and looked up in a half scowl from beneath lifted brows. "—was . . . a pair-fectly *mah*-vlous day!"

The President slapped his knee and laughed uproariously.

In the morning Mrs. Roosevelt rose early, as usual. She bathed and dressed in a beige knit dress with a thin brown leather belt, and placed a string of small, glittering quartz beads around her neck. She arrived at the President's bedroom as he was finishing his breakfast and scanning the last of the morning newspapers. It was her habit to spend fifteen minutes with him at this time of day. After she had said good-morning and asked how he felt, she invariably brought out a handful of notes about things she wanted to discuss with him. For the most part they would be requests of many kinds from people who wrote to her. Occasionally she urged on him a particular policy. She would draw a chair close to his bed, go over her notes, and scribble his answers on them.

The President would finish a bite or two of egg and a

bit of toast and sip his coffee, listening patiently—very often to requests he could not or did not want to grant.

This morning, at the end of their meeting, she told him about the body found in the Red Room. He didn't seem much interested. He asked her to be circumspect and to give him a report when she learned who the man was.

All he said that was of any significance was a sharp rebuke to the Secret Service. "Next door to a state dinner," he said. "While it was going on! It is intolerable."

She gave that word to Stanlislaw Szczygiel when he came to her office a little later. He apologized and said it was all but impossible to control the traffic through the public rooms of the White House.

"I can assure you," he said, "that the private quarters and the Executive Wing are safe. But the public rooms see hundreds of people every day, and we are still bound by the old tradition that the White House is a public building that the citizenry is entitled to visit."

"Very well," she said. "You had better see what can be done to improve matters, though. So—What do we know about the man found dead in the Red Room?"

"We know who he was," said Szczygiel. "And Lieutenant Kennelly will be here shortly with the autopsy report. Also, I spent some time last night and this morning interrogating the staff."

"Who was he, then?"

Szczygiel raised his brows and turned down the corners of his mouth. "A criminal," he said. "His name was Alekzandr Djaković, better known as Shondor Jack. His fingerprints, sent to the FBI central files, turned up quite a record."

He handed to Mrs. Roosevelt a small sheaf of green paper, and she read:

Djaković, Alekzandr, alias Shondor Jack.
b. 3/24/1876, Oradea, Austria-Hungary. Immigrated U.S., New York, 1903; naturalized U.S. cit., 1908.
Arrest 2/11/06, Cleveland PD, assault, dismissed.
Arrest 8/1/09, Cleveland PD, larceny, sent. 90 days, rel. 1/12/10.
Arrest 7/4/10, Toledo PD, burglary, sent. 10 to 25, rcvd. Ohio Pen. 9/19/10, parole 12/12/18.
Arrest 6/23/19, Cleveland PD, burglary, dismissed.
Arrest 8/13/19, Cleveland PD, assault, sen. 6 mos., rel. 3/2/20.
Arrest 4/11/20, Cleveland PD, theft, auto, dismissed.
Arrest 3/22/21, Prohibition Ag., transporting, dismissed.
Arrest 5/19/21, Prohibition Ag., transporting, U.S. Dist. Ct., probation 1 yr.
Arrest 8/19/21, Cleveland PD, burglary.
Probation revoked, committed Leavenworth Pen. 9/15/21, rel. 9/15/22.
Arrest 10/22/22, Cincinnati PD, murder 1st deg., acquitted 2/1/23.
Arrest 3/11/23, Cleveland PD, suspicious pers., dismissed.
Arrest 6/19/23, Cleveland PD, burglary, sent. 5 to 15, rcvd. Ohio Pen 8/7/23, parole 1/6/30.
Arrest 4/28/30, Cleveland PD, aggr. assault, dismissed.
Arrest 5/12/30, Cleveland PD, murder, acquitted.
Arrest 9/19/30, Cleveland PD, burglary, sen. 10 to 20.
Indicted 11/18/30, Habitual Criminals Act, sen. life.
Escape from custody, 12/30/30.

Wanted by Cleveland PD, Cuyahoga Co. sheriff, Ohio Pen. Subject often armed, to be considered dangerous.

Descr.—5′6″, 155 lb., eyes hazel, hair gray, knife scar between thumb and index finger right hand. Speaks with East-European accent. Subject heavy user alcohol, maybe reefers, gambles heavily on horses, consorts

> with prostitutes. May be living off earnings of one or more prostitutes. To be regarded chiefly a "cat burglar."

"When the record refers to dismissed charges . . . ?" asked Mrs. Roosevelt.

"It probably means he intimidated the only witness," said Szczygiel.

"Yes . . . He was no great loss to society, was he?"

"No, Ma'am. If he hadn't died in the White House, I'd be inclined to congratulate whoever did it and forget about it."

"But that would leave a murderer at large," said the First Lady.

"I suppose so. I—"

Her telephone rang. Lieutenant Kennelly was downstairs. She told the ushers to bring him up. She called the pantry and ordered coffee.

Lieutenant Edward Kennelly was no stranger to the White House. He had spent much time there during the struggle last year to solve the murder of Vivian Taliafero in the rose garden. Because the function of the Secret Service was to protect the President and his family, not to investigate crimes, the Service did not have such elementary resources as ballistics labs, autopsy rooms, fingerprint facilities—or even the personnel to do the pavement-pounding work of a criminal investigation. The Secret service relied on the District of Columbia police for most of these facilities.

Some of them might have been provided by the FBI, but the President emphatically did not trust the headline-chasing John Edgar Hoover and his clinging, cloying buddy Clyde Tolson.

Kennelly was a lifelong cop, an Irishman who had

earned his promotions and now was second-in-command in the District detective bureau. He was tall, with a pink, shiny face and white hair. He bowed to the First Lady and said it was an honor to see her again:

"Though I could wish it was not because of another one of these problems."

"It is a pleasure to see you again, Lieutenant Kennelly, in any circumstances," she said with a smile. "Have a chair. I have ordered some coffee."

Kennelly sat down facing the First Lady, who was seated at her desk. "I have the autopsy report," he said. "I'm afraid it doesn't add much to what we already know."

"Then just recite the basic facts," she said.

"The subject died between nine o'clock and nine-thirty last evening," said Kennelly. "He was stabbed in the back six times. He was also stabbed in the throat. It is not possible to tell whether he was stabbed in the throat first or last or between two of the other stabbings. In any case, the knife struck vital organs. There was massive internal bleeding."

"Stabbed in the throat . . ." Szczygiel mused. "That's different from his throat being cut."

"Yes," said Kennelly. "Also, his larynx was crushed, suggesting that he was maybe grabbed from behind, around the throat, then stabbed in the back."

"That would explain why no one heard him cry out," said Szczygiel.

"Besides that, musicians were playing in the State Dining Room," said Mrs. Roosevelt.

"There is one fact that seems a little unusual—or maybe not so unusual, depending on how you look at it," said Kennelly.

"What is that?"

"The blade of the knife was seven inches long," said Kennelly. "Not the kind a criminal might carry. More like a kitchen knife, a butcher knife. What's more, the wounds suggest it was extremely sharp. The wounds are deep, sure, but they're also long, suggesting that the blade cut through laterally as well as being plunged in."

"Well, then," said the First Lady. "Any suspects, Mr. Szczygiel?"

Stan Szczygiel shrugged. "We have to go at it methodically, Ma'am. That's all I know how to do."

3

"A . . . *methodical* investigation," the First Lady repeated, nodding. "Well, then. What questions have we to answer?"

She took a lined pad from her desk and began to write questions:

What was Mr. Jack doing in White House?
How did he get in, at night?
How did the killer get in?
Did the killer *have* to get in?
Did anyone in White House know Jack?
If not, then who killed him?
What motive?

"Just a few preliminary questions," she said. "Probably not in correct order."

Kennelly glanced over the questions. "When we have the answers to those," he said, "we'll have the murderer."

"Not necessarily," said Mrs. Roosevelt.

"I've done one or two things we may consider methodical," said Szczygiel. "As I mentioned before, Ma'am, I questioned the staff about who was in the White House last night."

"A very great number of people, I'm afraid," said the First Lady.

"Ah, but . . ." said Szczygiel. "The guests at the judiciary dinner were all formally dressed. None of them, I imagine, bore much resemblance to the potbellied Shondor Jack in his yellow-white suit."

"So who saw him?" she asked.

Szczygiel smiled and shrugged. "I'm afraid no one did. But there's a point. How did so conspicuous an intruder get into the White House and all the way to the Red Room, next door to the State Dining Room, on the occasion of a state dinner, without being seen?"

"With help," said Mrs. Roosevelt.

"Precisely," said he.

Kennelly frowned over the notepad and questions. "Makes sense," he said.

"All right," said Szczygiel. "A couple of the ushers and one of the housemaids saw two people walking through the halls last night. I mean people not formally dressed, not guests for the judiciary dinner. We can identify one of them. A man. A young woman . . . we cannot identify."

"Shondor Jack was not killed by a young woman," said Kennelly. "He was murdered by a strong man."

"Agreed," said Szczygiel. "So let me introduce a suspect."

"I always like to have a suspect in custody," said Kennelly. "It tidies things up so much."

"Well, I'm not sure we're ready to take this suspect into custody," said Szczygiel. "We don't have that much on him. But I think it's worth taking a look at the man and asking him a few questions." He turned to Mrs. Roosevelt and asked, "May I borrow your phone directory there?"

She handed him a pair of mimeographed sheets: the internal telephone directory of the White House, with the list of extension numbers. The switchboard knew most of the staff by name, but it was efficient to use the numbers.

"Uh—Excuse me," said Kennelly. "Can I see that?"

Szczygiel frowned. "The phone list?"

"Yeah, if you don't mind."

Kennelly took the mimeographed list and glanced over it quickly. "This is a White House phone directory? Doesn't say anything about the President. Doesn't say anything about how to call Mrs. Roosevelt."

"Those extension numbers are confidential," Szczygiel explained. "You want to speak to the President, you have to tell the switchboard operator, and she'll put you through to a secretary who'll have some questions to ask before she decides to ask Missy LeHand or Grace Tully if the President has time to talk to you."

Kennelly turned the sheets of paper over, as if he expected to see something on the back. "Damn . . ." he muttered. "Stupid of me not to have recognized what it was." He looked up and spoke directly to the First Lady. "Shondor Jack had these same sheets of paper, in his inside jacket pocket. White House telephone list. Fancy that."

"Add to our list of questions," she said.

How and why did Jack get WH phone list?

"Curious," murmured Szczygiel.

"In any event," said Mrs. Roosevelt, "who is the suspect whose name is on this list?"

"Asman," said Szczygiel. "A lawyer, as I understand. Works in the Executive Wing, for Mr. Hopkins." He squinted over the telephone list. "Ah . . . three eight three. Shall I, or . . . ?"

Mrs. Roosevelt handed him the telephone. "Make the call, Mr. Szczygiel," she said.

The coffee was delivered, along with a small assortment of Danish—unfortunately yesterday's. The First Lady and the two investigators sipped the coffee and chatted while they waited for the lawyer from the Executive Wing to come across and to the second floor.

He arrived. Christian Asman. Mrs. Roosevelt's first observation was that he seemed muscular enough to have grabbed a man around the throat from the rear and repeatedly plunged a butcher knife into his back. Muscular enough, yes. Beyond that, he was an early-middle-aged man of a bit more than medium height, his features unmemorable, except perhaps for his sandy-red hair. Although he was not smoking one now, she would observe later that he puffed tiny cigars and let the fumes trickle up behind the lenses of his gold-rimmed spectacles.

Asman was also, she noticed immediately, obsessively determined to ingratiate himself. He was *too* deferential.

She disliked making snap judgments about people, especially about people who might be suspected of something; but she quickly concluded that she simply could not like this man.

At her invitation he sat down, and at her further invitation he accepted a cup of coffee with cream and sugar.

"Mr. Asman," she said quietly, "are you aware that last night a man was murdered in the White House?"

He nodded. "I became aware of it when Mr. Szczygiel asked me this morning what I was doing in the White House in the middle of the evening."

"Yes. And your answer to the question was . . . ?"

Asman took a sip of coffee. "I work for Mr. Hopkins," he said. "I believe he will confirm that my duties often require me to be on the premises well beyond ordinary working hours. The legal problems of the Works Projects Administration are demanding and complex; but Mr. Hopkins often assigns me to unrelated work, like the judicial reform bill I am working on now."

"That places you in the Executive Wing," said Szczygiel. "It does not explain your presence in the White House itself after nine o'clock last night.

"My presence here is readily explained," said Asman with a precision and confidence in his voice that Mrs. Roosevelt found annoying. She wanted to be fair to this young man, but . . . He went on: "I came over to see if I could pick up a snack in the pantry. I often do when I work very late. By nine o'clock, a man does begin to think about the dinner he is missing."

"Your wife—"

"I am sorry, Ma'am," he interrupted quietly. "I have no wife. I am a bachelor. When I miss my dinner at my boarding house, I do think I am entitled to a sandwich from the White House pantry."

"Of course," said she. "So you came in from the Executive Wing at about what time?"

"Oh . . . Nine-fifteen perhaps. No later than nine-thirty."

"In fact," Szczygiel interrupted, "you came through the guard station between the Executive Wing and the White House at nine twenty-three."

Asman nodded. "I can't argue with that."

"But you never returned," said Szczygiel.

"No," said Asman with easy confidence. "They told me in the pantry that the judges were all upstairs, so I ate my sandwich in the downstairs hall and wandered up the stairs into the Cross Hall to catch a glimpse of the famous people. I saw them. I saw the justices of the Supreme Court. You know, when you're a lawyer—"

"Who did you see, Mr. Asman?" asked Mrs. Roosevelt.

"Well, obviously, a lawyer who hasn't pleaded cases before the Supreme Court doesn't know all the justices by sight. But I saw the chief justice, I am sure. And Mr. Justice Cardozo . . . Mr. Justice Brandeis . . . Mr. Justice—"

"Very well," said Mrs. Roosevelt. "But then you did not return to your office in the Executive Wing?"

"No. All the people were leaving onto the North Portico, so I just went out that way myself. I guess I left the lights on in my office, but . . . I suppose I thought everyone would excuse that."

"And then?" asked Kennelly.

Asman shrugged. "No limousine was picking *me* up. So I walked down the driveway and out onto Pennsylvania Avenue."

"And went home?" asked Mrs. Roosevelt.

"No, as a matter of fact. I went to the Farragut Bar, where I sometimes have a drink with friends after work. Unhappily, I didn't see anyone I knew there last night, so I left and went home."

"Where are you from, Mr. Asman?" asked the First Lady. "I mean, what do you regard as your home town?"

"Well, New York City, actually," he said. "I'm afraid I've never really put down roots. I spent most of my teen years in New York, in Manhattan, living in a half-dozen flats my parents rented. I don't mean to say we were poor. Just rootless."

"But you went to Harvard," said Szczygiel. "Your personnel file says you graduated from Harvard, then Harvard Law."

"Oh, yes," he said. "That gave me an identification. One I'd never had from a home town. Harvard . . ."

"And you wind up in the White House, working for Harry Hopkins," said Mrs. Roosevelt.

"I am proud of that, Ma'am," said Asman.

Szczygiel stared for a moment at Christian Asman, with the air of a man who suspects he is hearing a pack of lies but cannot quite put his finger on why. "Have you ever been in Cleveland, Mr. Asman?" he asked.

He was violating the cardinal rule of cross-examination, which is that you never ask a witness a question when you don't already know the answer. And know it confidently. He was groping.

"As a matter of fact, I have," said Asman. "When you take a train from New York to Chicago, you stop in Cleveland. Actually, I thought once of joining a law firm there. But there are no law firms in Cleveland. I mean, there are none but squalid little collections of cheap shysters. I couldn't imagine a Harvard lawyer accepting an affiliation in a contemptible little hole like Cleveland."

Mrs. Roosevelt frowned. "You seem to have a firm opinion of Cleveland," she said.

"Well . . . A man knows shabby when he sees it."

"Very well," said Mrs. Roosevelt. Her frown, directed to the other two interrogators, conveyed, she hoped, her disinclination to mention the name Jack. She had not been trained, as lawyers were, to avoid questions when you didn't know what the witness was going to answer; but some intuitive guide inside her told her not to ask.

"You were in the White House when a crime was committed here," said Szczygiel.

"Yes. The rumor is around."

"Do the President and me a favor," said Mrs. Roosevelt. "Deny the rumor."

Asman nodded.

Szczygiel added something more forceful. "You will deny the rumor, Asman," he said, "more as a favor to yourself than as a favor to the President and Mrs. Roosevelt. Do I make myself clear?"

Asman's nod amounted to a bow. "Entirely clear," he said. "And I suppose that a declaration of innocence and loyalty from me at this point would be useless."

"We will receive it, Mr. Asman," said the First Lady. "Why shouldn't we?"

Asman nodded at her. "Then I assure you," he said, "you have my word, absolutely, that I am personally committed to the President and loyal to him, and to Mr. Hopkins; and I had nothing whatever to do with any crime committed in the White House last night."

Mrs. Roosevelt could not help but smile at the intense

solemnity with which this statement was given. "Very well, Mr. Asman," she said. "I suppose you understand that we are compelled to question anyone whose presence in the White House last night was unusual."

"Of course," said Asman.

When he had left, she scribbled another note on her pad.

Mr. Asman says he saw Justice B.

"Curious," she said. "He says he saw Mr. Justice Brandeis. But Mr. Justice Brandeis was not here. Perhaps we should not attach too much significance to that, but it is an interesting fact, don't you think?"

Kennelly shook his head. "Yes . . . Yes. Interesting. But what in the world could have been the connection between Shondor Jack and Chris Asman? Think about that a minute. Djaković has been a fugitive from justice for almost seven years. God knows how he was living. On income earned by prostitutes?"

"Let's do a little guessing here," said Stan Szczygiel. "Suppose Asman, who says he's a bachelor, was seeing a girl who was being run by Shondor Jack. Then . . . Did he owe money? Had he abused her? Did Jack come to the White House to collect? To take revenge?"

"That's reaching, Mr. Szczygiel," said Mrs. Roosevelt.

"Whoever killed Djaković had reason," said Szczygiel. "It was nothing sudden, not an accidental encounter. Whether it was Asman or not—"

"I acknowledge that," said Szczygiel. "But murder in the White House is a different matter from murder on the street, or in a bar—especially when the victim is a person who has no business being here. Shondor Jack made his way into the mansion through our security system—however many holes it may have. He came here purposefully. Whoever killed him didn't just happen on him in the Red Room and say, 'My Lord, there's Shondor! I think I'll just stab him.' Whoever killed him had a knife. Not only that, he was carrying a kind of knife people don't ordinarily carry. He—"

"I grant all of that, Mr. Szczygiel. It doesn't really connect Mr. Asman to the murder."

Szczygiel shrugged. "No, I suppose it doesn't."

The First Lady glanced at her watch. "I'm afraid I have an appointment, gentlemen. I suggest you try to find out the identity of the young woman who also was seen in the corridors of the White House last evening."

The First Lady did in fact have a luncheon appointment, and she needed to give a few minutes to the morning mail and to sign two or three dozen letters. Also, she took a minute or so to review the weekly press summary prepared by her secretaries to give her a sense of what the newspapers were saying about her. She saw nothing very interesting. A few positive comments, to the effect that she made an effort to be in touch with America and acquire personal experience of the lives of its people.

The press comments coming in from the Ohio Valley were generally favorable. The *Wheeling Intelligencer* had run photos of her sloshing around in the mud in high rubber boots. The *Marietta Times* ran a picture of her getting out of her car and wading through muddy water to greet people. The *Cincinnati Enquirer* described her visit as "the usual mob-appeal appearance, chillingly similar to the Hitler parades through the streets of German cities." (The President had described Cincinnati as "the biggest city in the United States without a newspaper.")

In the South she was a "nigger-lover." In Chicago, the contemptible Bertie McCormick's *Tribune* called her a "Red." The Hearst papers . . . Well, William Randolph Hearst was at a loss to find new lies to print and relied on the old ones. That was the state of his mind: gone and soon to be forgotten.

She looked for something new in these press summaries but had learned by now that something new was seldom to be found.

In any case, the luncheon ahead of her promised to be pleasant.

For a few weeks she'd had on today's schedule an informal lunch with four Hollywood personalities—three of them among the biggest of 1936 and likely to be big again in 1937. Each was in his own way a little controversial. Maybe the Hollywood press agents who had arranged this meeting had supposed such an engagement with the First Lady would lend these personalities a new measure of respectability.

The first was W.C. Fields, one of America's favorite comic actors, yet a man notorious for his fondness for gin, also for his screen persona that detested dogs and children.

The second was Edward G. Robinson, a consummate actor, yet a man with a reputation that derived from his portraying cruel gangsters perhaps too well.

The third was Gary Cooper, an actor not very well

known but controversial because in some quarters his *Mr. Deeds Goes to Town* was perceived to have a Communist leaning.

The fourth guest was a young Austrian actress named Hedy Keisler. She had, it seemed, appeared some time ago in a Czech film called *Extase*—meaning "Ecstasy," in which, in one scene, she had run through a woods, quite naked. When she came to the United States, Hollywood had recognized her as an alluring and talented actress, had changed her name to Hedy Lamarr, and planned a glamorous career for her. Then—horrors!—prints of *Extase* began to show up in the States and to be run at a few small theaters, and the harpies of pure morals had begun to scold. Miss Lamarr's studio had timidly suggested that being received for luncheon with Mrs. Roosevelt might help to abate the fury that had arisen around the unhappy young woman.

Mrs. Roosevelt was sympathetic to all these people, especially poor Miss Keisler—Miss Lamarr.

They assembled at noon in the Private Dining Room, over a luncheon of tuna salad and iced tea.

Edward G. Robinson was perhaps the most surprising of the four guests. The First Lady had, of course, seen some of his gangster movies, and it was a revelation to find him an unassuming, soft-spoken man with a cultivated interest in art. He spoke of the flower paintings of Georgia O'Keeffe.

Gary Cooper was not an actor, she concluded. He created no new persona for the screen; he only played himself. Gary Cooper was not Longfellow Deeds; Longfellow Deeds was Gary Cooper—the shy, handsome, engaging man who sat at her table.

Similarly, Fields was Fields. Having heard, no doubt,

that he would be offered nothing alcoholic to drink at a White House luncheon, he had fortified himself liberally before arriving. He was by no means drunk, but he smelled of alcohol, and in person he was the same bulgy-nosed, mobile-faced man he played, with the same unique voice. He spoke with an elaborate deferential courtesy, prefacing almost every comment with something like, "It is of course only *my* opinion, but . . ."

And the actress was charming. If her little problem had not elicited Mrs. Roosevelt's sympathy, her personality certainly would. The young woman spoke in a small, lyrical voice, with the velvety accent of southern Germany and Austria.

"Ve haf found so varm a velcome in the United States," she said.

"Americans are very hospitable people," said Edward G. Robinson.

"And tolerant," added Mrs. Roosevelt. "The little controversy about your Czech film will die down. Don't you think so, Mr. Cooper?"

Gary Cooper's mouth seemed to be filled with tuna salad. His eyes opened wide, and his head bobbed in an emphatic nod. "Umm-mm," he murmured.

"Well, it's only my own opinion of course, but I haven't much respect for the legions of the so-called decent," said Fields. "Their posturing is *in*decent."

"In Europe, vas not thought so unusual to appear in nudity," said Hedy Lamarr.

"That represents a level of sophistication we should hope to attain in the States," said Robinson.

After the luncheon, the group walked out in the colonnade between the White House and the Executive Wing. Though it was a winter day, the sun was bright, and the press photographers took their pictures without flash. Each of the Hollywood people thanked the First Lady, then four press agents who had not been invited to the luncheon hurried up to offer their thanks, and suddenly the session was over. Mrs. Roosevelt waved good-bye as she walked back into the White House, and the film people were escorted to their cars by White House policemen.

The First Lady's thoughts had been on the murder of Mr. Alekzandr Djaković all day, sometimes even during that interesting luncheon hour. Now, returning to her own office, she asked Tommy Thompson, her private secretary, to call Stanlislaw Szczygiel.

When Szczygiel arrived a few minutes later, he had news. "We have, I believe, identified the young woman who was at large in the house last night. I am not sure it is of any significance, but—"

"Have you questioned her?"

"Not yet."

"Then, do you want to call her up here?"

Szczygiel frowned. "I am at your service, Ma'am," he said. "If you want to become personally involved in and identified with this investigation—"

"I wish to *help*, Mr. Szczygiel," she said. "I find I am sometimes able to offer the professional investigators the benefit of some little insights: the insights of an amateur, a lay person. Sometimes those insights have been helpful."

"I will never forget your insights in the Taliafero case," he said. "Also, Jerry Baines tells me you solved the mystery of the murder of Congressman Colmer—discovered how the murderer was able to leave the body in the Oval

Office with all the doors and windows locked from the inside."

"Where is Mr. Baines, incidentally?"

"On vacation," said Szczygiel. "He is in Florida, I believe."

"Anyway, unless you had rather we didn't, let's call this young woman to come up here."

Szczygiel accepted the telephone she offered him.

When he had finished his call, he said, "I asked Kennelly for a copy of the inventory—I mean, the inventory of things found on the person of the late Shondor Jack. Here it is."

She read aloud from the paper. "Cash, eight hundred twenty-nine sixty-five. I should think that eliminates robbery as a motive. One simple house key. No bill-fold or wallet. The money was in his pockets. No identifying papers of any kind. One short, heavy screwdriver. One four-inch length of lead sash weight. One White House telephone directory. One yellow pencil." She shook her head. "Suggestive of what, Mr. Szczygiel?"

"Of a burglar, according to Kennelly," said the Secret Service Agent. "The screwdriver and lead weight were burglar tools. He would insert the screwdriver blade in a keyhole, then palm the weight and hit the screwdriver handle with it. That would break the tumblers in most simple locks. The combination is sometimes called a slap-jack."

"Is that all it takes to break into a house?" she asked.

"Most houses," said Szczygiel. "You understand, I am not a policeman. This is what Kennelly says."

"When I cease to live in the White House," Mrs. Roosevelt said with a little smile, "and live in a home of my own, I shall see to it that better locks are installed."

"We could use better locks in the White House," said Szczygiel. "The locks on most doors, even in the executive offices in the West Wing, are nearly worthless—says Kennelly."

"More decorative than functional," she suggested.

He nodded. "In the White House itself," he said. "Beautiful brass antiques. In the Executive Wing . . . Well, Kennelly's word for them is 'cheap.' "

In a few more minutes a young woman arrived. Margaret Dempsey. She was an exceptionally attractive young woman, in a modest way that met with Mrs. Roosevelt's instinctive approval. She appeared never to have been touched by a hairdresser or cosmetologist and wore her dark-brown hair simply combed, her brows unplucked, her skin untouched by rouge or even powder. If she wore any makeup, it was a faint touch of lipstick, so artfully applied that one could not really tell if it was there at all. She was simply dressed, as well, in a dark-green sweater and black skirt.

"Sit down, my dear," said Mrs. Roosevelt. "I hope we don't alarm you by asking you to respond to a few questions about last evening."

The young woman was completely calm. She looked at Mrs. Roosevelt with steady blue eyes and waited for the first question.

"Miss Dempsey is a lawyer," said Szczygiel.

"Indeed," said Mrs. Roosevelt, surprised.

"On the White House staff," said Szczygiel.

"Of *course*! I recall hearing the President say we had a young woman lawyer on the staff. Working for—"

"The NRA," said Margaret Dempsey quietly. "Originally. Then, when the Court struck it down, I was not sent home but was transferred to the Executive Wing. I am counsel to Mr. Corcoran."

"She's modest," said Szczygiel. "I looked at her personnel file. She graduated from Harvard Law in nineteen thirty-four and came to Washington on the emphatic personal recommendation of Professor Frankfurter. When the NRA staff began to disperse, Frankfurter wrote to Attorney General Cummings, urging that her services not be lost. So—"

"I thought," said Margaret Dempsey softly, "that working in the White House would be more interesting than working at the Department of Justice. Technically, Mr. Corcoran is head of the Reconstruction Finance Corporation, and technically I am one of his staff lawyers."

"Technically . . ." Mrs. Roosevelt laughed. "I imagine, Miss Dempsey, you know what my husband calls Mr. Corcoran."

The young woman nodded. "Tommy the Cork," she said.

"Yes. They are very close. That's why he has an office here—and you do."

"Almost all my work is highly confidential," said Margaret Dempsey.

"We needn't ask about it," said Mrs. Roosevelt. "What we do need to know is why you were in the White House last evening, after nine o'clock."

"I often work late," said Margaret Dempsey.

"In your office in the West Wing," said Szczygiel. "Granted." But some interrogation of staff places you in the White House itself, after nine last night. You have been here so infrequently that we had substantial difficulty in identifying you. And when we did, we saw that you had not entered the White House through the door between the colonnade and the House, the usual way of entering from the West Wing. You did not check in at the guard station there."

She shrugged. "I was tired. I walked out into the colonnade and decided I liked the cold winter air. You know. No cigarette smoke. No—I don't know what it is. What makes the air in some parts of the White House stink? A hundred years of dead bugs in the heating system? Anyway, I was glad to be out in the cold air, and I just came around and in through the North Portico. I said hello to the policeman on duty, but he wasn't taking names. I walked in. Did I break a rule?"

Mrs. Roosevelt shook her head. "Miss Dempsey . . . *why* did you need to enter the White House after nine last night?"

"I was looking for Chris Asman. He'd left his office and hadn't dropped off a file he was supposed to leave for me. His lights were still on, so I supposed he'd come over into the White House to pick up a sandwich in the pantry, which he often does when he works late. Frankly, I'd rather buy a hotdog off a street vendor than eat what your Mrs. Nesbitt cooks for the White House. Anyway, I came over, thinking I might see him. If I didn't, that was okay too. I went down to the pantry. He wasn't there. So, I walked back upstairs and out the North Portico, and left the White House. The cop smiled and waved as I went."

While the young woman made this statement, Stan Szczygiel frowned over her personnel file. "Miss Dempsey," he said. "I see here that your home town is Rocky River, Ohio. Is that not a suburb of Cleveland?"

"If you want to know," she said, "if I ever met Shondor Jack, the answer is no."

"Tell us who Shondor Jack is, Miss Dempsey," said Mrs. Roosevelt.

The young woman smiled wryly. "He is the man who was murdered in the Red Room last night. The White House is not the best place in the world to keep secrets."

"You did not, of course, know such a person."

"Shondor Jack," said Margaret Dempsey. "Anyone who ever lived in Cleveland knows the name. There are lots of bodies still at the bottom of Lake Erie, put there by Shondor Jack."

4

The First Lady left the White House at six forty-five that Thursday evening to attend a dinner of labor leaders and their wives sponsored by the International Ladies Garment Workers Union. She would be the principal speaker, and as she was dressing she hastily reviewed the text of the speech she had written two or three days earlier.

As she left her bedroom she met the President, who was just being wheeled into the West Sitting Hall by his valet. Missy LeHand was walking beside him.

“Making a speech, are you?” the President asked, probably referring to his observation that she was wearing the same white gown she had worn to the judiciary dinner.

“Yes. I shall be rather late returning, I imagine.”

“Have you finished the Red Room business?”

She shook her head. “No. Not at all. It is really quite distressing. The man was a wanted felon.”

The President nodded, then shrugged, as she walked

on toward the elevator. His mood was somber for a moment, then abruptly brightened as he saw the cart with the cocktail things waiting for him. "Well," he said. "Who's home?"

"Pa is here, I think," said Missy. She meant General Edwin Watson, the President's military aide.

"Well, let's get him up here," said the President as he wheeled himself into place beside the cocktail cart. "And Harry the Hop. I know he's still in his office."

These were friends: Missy, Pa, and Harry. They were people who entertained the President with cheerful conversation, who knew that this hour was not the time to raise problems. Missy was always sensitive to his moods. She understood Franklin Roosevelt, was devoted to him, and adjusted her own moods to accommodate his. Big, gruff Pa Watson was a treasury of jokes and stories and knew when the President wanted to hear them. Harry Hopkins was a dedicated man, but he knew how and when to relax.

While they waited, the President and Missy sat quietly under the windows at the very west end of the White House and stared down the long center hall of the second floor, all the way to the window at the east end.

Shortly the friends were assembled. The President shook his martinis: always measured with the precision of a careful pharmacist and shaken until the clear fluid was colder than the ice, if that was possible; always poured into chilled stem glasses. The President drank two, occasionally three, every evening. Pa would join him in martinis this evening. Missy preferred Scotch, Harry bourbon.

"Do you realize what we did last evening?" the President asked with a broad smile as he lit a Camel. "How good is your history? Who remembers the Duchess of Richmond's ball?"

"On the eve of the Battle of Waterloo," said Pa Watson. "Wellington was guest of honor, and it is said that one of Napoleon's generals was there incognito, that in effect Wellington entertained an enemy general on the evening before the great battle."

Hopkins laughed. "The story is that Napoleon's man was dressed as a Belgian officer. Wellington is supposed to have said to him, "We'll have sharp work tomorrow,' or something like that."

"Exactly," said the President. "Last night we entertained the justices of the Supreme Court. Tomorrow morning I am announcing a court-reform bill that will set them back on their heels for good and sure."

"Is that why you've called in the secretarial staff for six-thirty AM?" Missy asked.

"Yes. They've got to cut mimeograph stencils. I'm handing the bill and supporting documents to the Cabinet and leaders of Congress at ten o'clock, to the press at ten-thirty."

"Exactly what are you proposing?" asked Pa Watson.

Harry Hopkins had a general idea of what was coming. Missy and Pa did not.

The President smiled happily. "As you know," he said, "the Constitution says there shall be a Supreme Court. It doesn't say how many justices there shall be. We have nine now, but there haven't always been nine. I am proposing that the Congress increase the size of the Court: one new justice for every sitting justice over the age of seventy. Unless some of the sitting justices retire, that will make six new seats. And I will be able to appoint men who won't find constitutional objections to everything we try to do."

"Wow . . ." said Pa. He shook his head. "I'd just as soon we hadn't mentioned Waterloo."

When the order came down from the West Sitting Hall to send up two dozen oysters on the half shell, Stan Szczygiel was sitting in the kitchen, talking with Mrs. Henrietta Nesbitt, the housekeeper.

"You need to talk with Joyce," she said.

"Joyce . . . ?"

"Oh, I don't try to know their last names. One of the Negroes. She works here evenings. She'd of been here."

"Where is she now?"

Mrs. Nesbitt looked at the clock. "Due," she said.

"Let me ask you something else," he said. "Is there a butcher knife missing?"

"Not that I know of. Henry! You know if any knife is missing?"

Henry was a tall, light-skinned black. He moved with graceful dignity and opened a drawer in the big table in the center of the room. He ran his finger back and forth as if he were counting, and he began to shake his head.

"Can't say there is, Miz Nesbitt," he said.

Szczygiel looked into the drawer. It was filled with a jumble of knives of all sizes, plus sharpening stones and steels. None of the knives was new. Some of them had been sharpened so often that their blades were worn away in long arcs. But there were so many it would have been difficult for the man to say if a knife were missing.

Szczygiel lifted a butcher knife from the drawer and tested its edge with his finger. "Somebody keeps these damned sharp," he said.

"Yes, suh," said Henry. "Some folks is fanatics 'bout it."

"You know, Henry, that a man was stabbed to death in the White House last night," said Szczygiel.

"Suh," said Henry, "when I came to work at the White House, I was told with a whole lot of emphatic that the most important thing is to keep your eyes and ears shut, don't see nothin', don't hear nothin', then you can't say nothin' you shouldn't. So . . . maybe somebody did say something 'bout somebody being stabbed; but I was tryin' not to hear, so I didn't really catch it."

Szczygiel smiled. "That's fine, Henry. And you were questioned a little this morning about who you saw and what you saw."

"Yes, suh. Nearly scared my wife to death to have that young agent come to my house. But, like I said, I didn't see nothin' unusual last night. They wanted to know 'bout nine o'clock and like that. I was scrapin' dishes, washin' dishes, cleanin' up after that big dinner. I was busy right here and didn't go out of the kitchen."

"Here is Joyce," said Mrs. Nesbitt in a thin voice that was meant to suggest Joyce should have arrived sooner.

Joyce Carter was a handsome, diminutive, young black woman, dressed in the uniform of a maid: black dress, white apron. Her duties in the White House, as Szczygiel already knew, included work in the kitchen and carrying food and drinks to the floors above, as ordered. Usually food orders were taken up by the butler, but when he was already on an errand, Joyce Carter could go anywhere in the White House.

"We couldn't reach you to question you earlier," said Szczygiel. "You weren't at home today."

The young woman spoke softly but firmly. "When I leave the White House after work, I have a private, personal life," she said.

"Sleep with some buck, do you?" asked Mrs. Nesbitt scornfully.

Joyce Carter flared, ready to respond angrily, but Szczygiel intervened curtly. "That will be *all*, Mrs. Nesbitt," he said coldly. "When I require further information from you, I will let you know. I want to speak with Miss Carter alone."

"I—"

"Good . . . evening . . . Mrs. . . . Nesbitt."

The housekeeper swung around and stalked off. Szczygiel winked at Joyce Carter.

"I'm going to call you Joyce," he said. "So you can call me Stan."

The young woman, surprised, nodded. "Okay."

"Now. Between nine and nine-thirty last night, a man was murdered in the Red Room. It was done by a strong man, who stabbed the victim repeatedly. Obviously, then, you are not a suspect. And all I want to know is what you saw. If anything."

"Like did I see somebody in the White House that didn't belong here?" she said.

"Right."

Joyce Carter pondered for a long moment. Then she shook her head. "I can't say I saw anybody. Anybody unusual. Didn't see anybody you wouldn't expect."

"Where were you, Joyce?"

"I was here most of the time. That big dinner last night was served by men, mostly. One time, they ran short of butter, and I took up a tray."

"Were you scraping plates, washing dishes?"

Her chin rose. "No. I'm a *maid*. I serve. I don't clean up."

"Did you take oysters to the second floor last night?"

She smiled. "Mr. Hopkins. He loves oysters."

Szczygiel paused and drew a deep breath. He disliked mentioning a name. He would rather the name came from the person being questioned. But—"Joyce," he said. "Do you know who Christian Asman is?"

"Yes, sir. He's a lawyer, over in the West Wing. He comes over for sandwiches now and then."

"Last night?"

"Yes."

"Tell me as much as you can about it. When did he come, what did he say, what did he do, how long was he here . . . ?"

She considered for a moment. "He came into the kitchen about . . . oh, say quarter after nine. Kind of grinning. Asked for sandwiches, as usual."

"As usual?"

"Well, he works late. Misses his dinner. So he came in and asked me if I'd make him a couple of sandwiches. I do it about half the time he comes in. Sometimes Henry makes them for him. Anyway, he sat down and—"

"Where did he sit?"

"Right there," she said, pointing at the chair at the table that faced the knife drawer.

"Could he have taken a knife from the drawer while you were making his sandwiches?" asked Szczygiel.

Her eyes widened. "Oh, I see where this is going," she said. "Stan, I don't want to make trouble for Asman, but . . . Well, yes, he could have lifted a knife from that drawer when I wasn't looking. I went to the refrigerator to get some ham and cheese. He could—Oh, yeah. Jesus!"

"Okay," said Szczygiel. "It doesn't prove anything. Not anything, really. Now. You say he comes in for sandwiches from time to time. Was there anything different about last night?"

She thought about that, then shrugged. "Sometimes he takes his sandwiches back to his office. Sometimes he eats them here. Last night he ate them here. I gave him a bottle of beer. I knew he'd want that. He sat right there and ate his sandwiches and drank his beer."

"No hurry?"

"No hurry."

"So, how long was he here, all told?"

"How long does it take to eat two sandwiches and drink a bottle of beer?"

Szczygiel glanced around the kitchen. At this time of the evening there was almost no activity. A little later they would prepare the President's dinner tray and take it up to the second floor. Usually they took a tray for Miss LeHand, too. Vegetables lay in simmering pots of water, losing every semblance of flavor. Meat waited to be shoved into an oven and hurriedly heated. The White House kitchen had more the air of a soup kitchen than that of the kitchen in which meals were prepared for the President of the United States.

"Joyce . . . Is there anything more you can tell me about Chris Asman?"

She stared at him for a moment. She shrugged. "He . . . He has sometimes propositioned me," she said.

"He what?"

"He asked me to go to bed with him."

* * *

On the second floor, the cocktail things had been cleared from the West Sitting Hall. The lights had been dimmed. The President had bathed and been helped to bed. He sat propped against a stack of pillows, smoking a Camel, and scanning the final drafts that would be mimeographed in the morning.

Missy entered. She wore a light-blue nightgown under a sheer peignoir. Without a word, she picked up the telephone and called the kitchen. Their dinner trays would be up in a few minutes.

The President put aside the papers he had been reading. "Some music?" he asked quietly, wearily—letting Missy see what others almost never saw: that he was tired.

She bent over him and kissed him lightly on the forehead, then turned on the radio and worked the tuning dials until she found a concert. Somewhere an orchestra was playing "L'Aprés-midi d'un Faune," and the President smiled.

Their trays were brought. The food was unappetizing, and they only picked at it and shortly pushed their trays aside.

"You love a good fight," she said to him.

He nodded.

"Well, you're picking one. In the morning you're going to have one hell of a fight on your hands."

His quiet, solemn, private mood turned a little toward his public ebullience—but only a little. "I believe in what I'm going to try to do," he said. "And the fight—Well, Missy, if I didn't have a tough fight sometimes, for what I believe in, I don't think I could endure this place." He turned a hand toward their dinner trays, then opened both hands toward the bedroom of the President of the United States. It was no more impressive than a bedroom in a modest railroad hotel. "Could you?" he asked.

A tear ran down Missy's cheek. "If it weren't for being with you, Boss, I wouldn't even *visit* this place."

He reached for her hand. Then he altered the mood of the conversation. "You know what they say about Washington," he said, reaching over with his other hand to put a finger under her chin and raise her face toward his. "It has all the warm charm of New York, coupled with the efficiency of New Orleans."

Stan Szczygiel had his dinner at Ford's, a restaurant where you sat on a stool at a counter, examined the menu, and wrote your own order on a slip. Then, often as not, the waitress would ask you what you had ordered, because she could not read. The dinner was filling—pot roast well done, mashed potatoes and gravy, lima beans, one slice of bread with one pat of butter, and coffee, all for thirty cents. The options were chicken or swiss steak instead of pot roast, tea instead of coffee, price the same. Service was quick, and you were expected to eat fast.

Walking out onto Fourteenth Street afterward, he found Ed Kennelly waiting at the curb in an unmarked black Ford coupe. Stan climbed in on the passenger side.

"Anything?" he asked.

"He left the White House at seven," said Kennelly.

"And?"

"Ate dinner at Child's. Blue-plate special."

"And?"

"He's at the Farragut Bar. The boys watched him go in. He hasn't come out."

"Have they gone in?"

"Just long enough to be sure he's there."

"What do we do?" asked Szczygiel. "Go have a look?"

"Why not?"

Kennelly pulled a microphone off a hook under the Ford's dashboard, and Szczygiel watched with fascination as the detective talked back and forth with his headquarters without having to get out and go to a call box.

"Car two-two calling HQ. Two-two calling HQ."

"This is HQ. Go ahead, two-two."

"Two-two is leaving last call station to proceed to Farragut Bar. Is there any word from our guys there?"

"Uh . . . No word, two-two. Not since your last call."

"Okay, two-two is proceeding to Farragut Bar and will be there until further word."

"Gotcha, two-two. Whatcha think about snow? Look like we're gonna get any tonight?"

Kennelly shook his head. "How the hell can I tell? The sky is dark."

"Gotcha. And thanks."

Kennelly glanced at Szczygiel as he hung up the microphone. "Sometimes they ask for a ball score," he said. "What they think this is out here?"

"First I ever saw of anything like it," said Szczygiel. "Radio car. I've heard of it but never saw it. Could be damned useful some time."

The Farragut Bar was on Eye Street, not far from Farragut Square. It had long been a favorite watering hole for New Deal staffers: not far from the White House, but far enough that the bosses were not expected to drop in. It had the look of an old pre-Prohibition saloon or a speakeasy, both of which it had been. Many customers sat on stools at the handsome, carved-oak bar that ran almost the whole length of the tavern. Other customers sat around a score of tables. Brass lamps and little more conveyed the nautical theme the place's name suggested. Better than the décor were the costumes worn by the two bartenders and four waitresses: imitation naval uniforms with white jackets and nautical caps for the men, and the same white jackets and caps, plus thigh-high blue skirts for the women.

Szczygiel and Kennelly stood for a moment in the door, accustoming their eyes to the dim lights, and their noses and throats to the thick cigarette smoke in the air. Kennelly had been there before, so the atmosphere was no surprise to him. Szczygiel had not, and while it was no surprise, it was a revelation of how the New Deal crowd amused themselves after hours.

It was obvious, too, that a few young women were working the bar, looking for quick dollars from brief pleasure.

"Be damned!" said Szczygiel.

"Uh?"

Szczygiel nodded toward a table halfway along the length of the bar. "Look at that! You know the guy? I mean the one with the chippie hanging all over him. You know him?"

Kennelly shook his head.

"Hey!" Szczygiel grunted. "You and I are faithful sons of the Church, are we not? Damned right! Well, turn the collar around on that son of a bitch and you'll know him. That's Coughlin! Charles Coughlin. The radio priest! The rabid anti-Roosevelt guy! Radio League of the Little Flower. Priest, my achin' backside! And that's Congressman Lemke, the sucker Coughlin and Gerald L.K. Smith ran for President, right beside him!"

Kennelly squinted into the smoky gloom. He shook his head. "I can't be sure . . ."

"Wanta walk over and ask?"

"Szczygiel!" Kennelly grunted. "You've been in Washington a long time. Things happen. People do what people do. We're not here to change it. We're not here to trumpet scandal."

Szczygiel stood stiffly for a moment, drawing a deep breath and staring balefully at the obviously-drunk Coughlin. "Well . . ." he said finally. "Drew Pearson could make a fortune in here."

"What makes you think he *doesn't* make a fortune in here?" asked Kennelly. "How innocent can you be, Stan?"

"I want to retire," said Szczygiel glumly. "I don't want to have to . . . Where's Asman?"

"Over there," said Kennelly. He had not been much distracted by what they had seen and had looked around for and found Christian Asman at a table toward the rear of the Farragut.

Szczygiel stared through the smoky atmosphere of the bar and also spotted Asman, seated at a table with an exquisitely beautiful young blonde woman, wearing a pink knit dress.

"Who is she?"

Kennelly shrugged. "I haven't the faintest idea. I can't say I know every hooker in town, but I don't recognize her."

"May not be a hooker," said Szczygiel. "My God, man—"

"Okay. There are hookers in here, plenty. But not every girl in the joint is a hooker, that's true."

Stan Szczygiel squinted at Asman and the blonde for a long moment. "What do we do, Ed?" he asked.

"Detective work . . ." said Kennelly. "It takes a hell of a lot of patience. The guy that moves in too quick loses the game. Let's have a beer and keep watch. Who knows what might happen?"

They pushed in between two men at the bar and ordered drinks—a beer for Kennelly, a gin for Szczygiel.

"Hey . . . you guys . . . FBI, aren't ya?" asked one of the men they had elbowed aside to reach the bar. "Know one when I see one. Where y' hats?"

"Actually," said Kennelly, "we work for John L. Lewis, the United Mine Workers."

The drunk stepped back and blinked as he stared at them. "Lewis . . . Y'don't mean it! By golly! John L.— Hey! I'd sworn you was law-type guys."

Kennelly smiled. "Never can tell, can ya?"

"I don' like your boss . . . but what the hell?"

Szczygiel tried not to be conspicuous about staring at Asman and the young woman. He had to admit she did not look like a prostitute. To the contrary, except that he saw her in a noisy, smoky bar, he would have taken her for a finishing-school grad, the daughter of some well-off businessman.

She sat with her legs crossed at the ankles. Her skirt covered her knees and some inches below. She smoked her cigarette by ladies' rules: never holding it between her lips, only between her fingers, and blowing her smoke away from her companion.

On the other hand, she violated the ladies' rule about never publicly showing affection for a man. Asman caressed her left hand, which lay on the table. Szczygiel noticed that Asman did not confine himself to stroking the back of her hand; he slipped his fingers under and caressed her palm. She not only accepted that intimate, even faintly erotic, caress; she closed her fingers around his and squeezed from time to time.

"Police work makes a man feel like a snoop sometimes," said Kennelly. "I mean, that could be completely innocent."

Szczygiel nodded. "So do we go home and forget it?"

Kennelly beckoned to the bartender and pointed at their two glasses. "Let's watch a little," he said.

They finished their second round of drinks and were standing at the bar unsure of whether to order a third when Asman and the girl rose abruptly and walked toward the door.

Kennelly and Szczygiel followed, ignoring the elaborate goodbye being pronounced by the drunk who thought they worked for John L. Lewis.

They reached the unmarked Ford by the time Asman had gotten a taxi.

It was easy to follow the taxi, which traveled only a mile or so north and west and stopped in front of a small, handsome brick house in Georgetown. Asman took the girl to the door while the taxi waited, and in the greenish glow of a gas mantel he kissed her goodnight—more fervently than her Georgetown neighbors might have approved.

Kennelly drove on after the taxi, to see if Asman were going home or had some other appointment. He picked up the radio microphone and spoke to headquarters, giving the Georgetown street address and asking them to find out who lived there.

Five minutes later, when they had followed the taxi back into downtown Washington, the radio dispatcher reported:

"Lieutenant, your street address is the residence of Senator John Fisher of Arkansas."

"Okay, thanks."

Kennelly glanced at Szczygiel. "Do you suppose that was the senator's daughter?"

"If the senator *has* a daughter," said Szczygiel.

"Yeah . . . A senator's daughter. Southern belle. Hmm."

"I'm not sure there's any significance in Asman's dating a senator's daughter," said Szczygiel. "I'm not sure there's any point in following him around town."

"What other suspect we got?" asked Kennelly as he lit a cigarette. "We might as well follow this one. Unless you're too tired and sleepy."

"Follow him," Szczygiel grunted.

This time the taxi stopped in front of the Gayety Burlesque. Asman got out, paid the driver, and stood for a moment in the bright lights of the facade. He seemed to hesitate for a moment, then went in.

"So," said Szczygiel as Kennelly pulled the car to the curb in a no-parking zone. "Gonna take in a show."

"Didn't you notice something unusual?" asked Kennelly.

"Like what?"

"Like that he didn't buy a ticket. He just walked in. He didn't even glance at the ticket taker, and the ticket taker just stared at him as he walked by."

"And the significance of that might be . . . ?"

"I don't know. I think I'd like to know. It could have nothing at all to do with Shondor Jack. Or it might. If Jack was living off the earnings of some girl, this is as likely a place to find her as any."

"So what do we do?"

"What I'm gonna do is go in the Gayety Bar there, next door, and have a beer. We stand near the front, we can watch the sidewalk through the window."

Szczygiel shrugged. "Does your job usually take you into so many bars?"

"Usually not ones as good as these two tonight. My line of work gets me into some real first-class neighborhoods."

Szczygiel glanced around the Gayety Bar. "You must see some real dives," he said. "This place doesn't impress me much."

"This is the kind of place where you find what you're looking for," said Kennelly.

Maybe so. Looking around, Szczygiel could see the routine here. The performers from the burlesque theater came in through a rear door, probably one that connected with backstage, and sat at the bar for a drink between one performance and the next. The girls were easily distinguishable by their heavy makeup and their exaggerated hair styles. The comics came in wearing their grotesque, baggy-pants costumes and painted-on faces. At the bar, most of the girls were joined by men. Some of them looked like pimps; others, like swains.

Kennelly spoke to the bartender. "Last show?" he asked.

The bald, cigar-chewing bartender nodded. "Running over for the finale in a minute. They'll all go on stage with the star, take their bows, and it's over for the night."

"Who's the star?"

"You walked past the joint and didn't see the signs? This month the star of the Gayety is Stormy Skye. Haven't ya been in to see her? Hey, man! Go over tomorrow night and get an eyeful of that broad! Prime stuff!"

"She be in here after the show?"

"Sometimes. But you won't see her the same way. You wanta see her in the skin."

All the performers hurried out the rear door. Szczygiel and Kennelly kept close watch on the street outside the window, waiting for Asman to come out. But he was not in the crowd that gathered on the sidewalk.

"Here y' go," said the bartender, nodding toward the rear of the bar.

The star of the Gayety Burlesque entered, on the arm of Christian Asman.

She was a tall blonde, the sort of young woman the posters outside the theater called "statuesque." Since she was a blonde, her publicity would also call her "bombastic." Other words that would be used about her were "voluptuous" and "enticing." She had already lit a cigarette, which hung from a corner of her mouth; and her sweat had made her eye makeup run. Szczygiel wondered what she would look like without makeup, with her hair washed out. A not-bad-looking girl, he guessed.

Disregarding her disheveled appearance, Chris Asman held Stormy firmly and guided her to a table at the rear of the room. He was smoking a thin little cigar, and he led his striptease star as if she were the most cherished of delicate ladies.

They sat down, and in a moment were joined by two of the baggy-pants comics, recognizable though now out of costume and makeup. The comics seemed to be paid more deference—if in fact any of these people were shown such an honor—than the star stripper. The lesser strippers, recognizable too, hovered around them, caressing their necks, offering them lights.

"Those guys, believe it or not, run the show," Kennelly explained. "Except for Stormy there, the star, the rest of the troupe is assembled around the comics. It's a travelling show. They'll move together from Washington to wherever. The comics are the organizers and make the contracts. The lesser girls have jobs or don't have jobs, depending on if the comics like them."

"A subculture, I think the word is," said Szczygiel.

Kennelly nodded. "Whatever that means. Anyway . . . what's Asman got to do with it? That's a closed little group, and they've taken him in."

"You figure Shondor Jack was once the business manager?" asked Szczygiel.

"Like to know," said Kennelly.

An hour later, Chris Asman led his star, Stormy Skye, out of the bar and to a taxi. Kennelly and Szczygiel followed them in the unmarked Ford. Asman took her home—that is, to his flat. Kennelly insisted on sitting on the street and keeping watch until the lights went out.

5

"It would be most unfair to attribute anything . . . *criminal* to this young woman," said Mrs. Roosevelt to Stan Szczygiel. "After all, we—"

It was difficult for her to focus on the Shondor Jack murder case now that she knew what was going on in the Oval Office. She knew—

Yes. Franklin had elected not to trust even her. He had trusted almost no one, apparently. Not even Missy. Not until the last moment, anyway. The mimeographed bill and supporting statements had been delivered to her only this morning, before she was awake—and that was an early hour indeed. Sitting in bed, she had scanned the documents; then—perceiving the vital importance of what she was reading—she had studied them intently.

She did not at all disagree with what he was trying to do. The mossback conservatives on the Supreme Court, holdovers from the administrations of Harding, Coolidge, and Hoover, had frustrated the new popular majority at every turn. Franklin was frustrated politically. She was frustrated philosophically, compelled to wonder whether the Constitution of the United States even made it impossible to enact legislation limiting the hours twelve-year-old children could work underground in coal mines.

But . . . Since 1933, the newspapers had constantly accused Franklin D. Roosevelt of wanting to scrap the Constitution and establish a Rooseveltian dictatorship. Now—Now he proposed to reconstitute the Supreme Court!

As much as she hoped this might be achieved, she had to worry that it would be taken as confirmation of every vicious accusation that had been made. Oh . . . Franklin had thrown down a gauntlet he might be forced to kneel and pick up himself!

The congressional leaders were in the Oval Office now, receiving their copies. In fifteen minutes the documents would be handed out at a press conference.

She . . .

"There is something criminal in there," said Szczygiel. He had no idea what was distracting the First Lady from the FBI document. "Please, ma'am, read the sheet."

She read another one of the distressing criminal records:

Schmidt, Gertrude, alias Gerty Smith, alias Betty Smith, alias La Storme, alias Busty Browne, alias Hotsy Totsy, alias Stormy Skye.

b. 4/19/07, Elkins, W.Va..

Arrest 8/21/21, Charleston, W. Va., PD, morals. Ref. Juv. Ct., probation.

Arrest 5/5/22, Wheeling, W.Va., morals, juv., committed 5/24/22, rel. 4/20/25.

Arrest 11/1/29, Cleveland PD, morals, sent. 90 days, rel. 2/11/30.
Arrest, 4/3/30, Cleveland PD, indecent exp., probation.
Arrest, 8/21/30, Cleveland PD, morals, sent. 6 mos., rel. 2/20/31.
Arrest 4/8/31, Cincinnati PD, morals, escaped, wanted.
Arrest 7/14/36, LA PD, indecent exp., held for Cincinnati PD, Cincinnati, charge dropped, released 8/02/36.

"Notice," said Szczygiel, "the Cleveland connection. She was in Cleveland in nineteen twenty-nine and thirty. So was Shondor Jack. And she left Cleveland about the time he did."

"Coincidence?" asked the First Lady. "After all, Cleveland is a big city."

"Yes, Ma'am," he said. "It could very well be nothing but a coincidence. On the other hand, when you add two coincidences together—"

"The other coincidence being?"

"The other coincidence being that our only suspect in the murder of Djaković has an intimate relationship with this woman."

"I'm not sure it's significant, Mr. Szczygiel," she said.

"Neither am I. Not sure, that is. But I'm developing a stronger interest in our friend Chris Asman."

"Not, I hope, to the exclusion of pursuing other leads."

"Frankly, we have no other leads," said Szczygiel. "But Mr. Asman has unconventional personal habits. When he left his office last night, he dined alone, then went to the Farragut Bar, where he met Miss Joan Fisher, the daughter of the senator from Arkansas. They were more than friendly. He took her home in a cab, and then he went to the Gayety and picked up the stripteaser. And he took her home for the night. Apart from that, he has propositioned one of the colored maids here in the White House."

"Oh, Mr. Szczygiel, are you sure?"

"Unless the girl is lying. And why would she do that?"

"Why, indeed?"

"While Asman is in his office today, Lieutenant Kennelly is going to search his flat."

Mrs. Roosevelt's face hardened. "I am always opposed to that sort of thing," she said. "I am opposed, that is, unless we have much more evidence against a suspect than we have against Mr. Asman."

"I'm afraid Kennelly is proceeding on his own," said Szczygiel.

Never had the President been in better form. His Cabinet and the leaders of the House and Senate were assembled in the Oval Office. Missy LeHand and Grace Tully moved among them, handing out sets of mimeographed documents. So freshly made were these documents that the air in the room smelled of mimeograph ink.

Animated and genial, the President made no statement, only greeted the various congressional leaders and made happy quips. He gave them no time to question him, saying he would like to, but his press conference was beginning immediately. He saluted them all, thanked them for coming, and with a cheery wave let himself be wheeled out of the office.

He was confident the Congress would pass his court-reform bill. He might not have been so confident if he had overheard the comment made by the elderly chairman of the House Judiciary Committee, who had been a faithful supporter of the President. But now, as the chairman folded his documents, he looked up and shook his head. "Boys," he said, "here's where I cash in my chips."

Kennelly saw no one as he walked into the little apartment block on M Street. He didn't have to show his badge or give anyone an indication as to why he was there. He knew which flat was Asman's. He had watched the lights come on and go off in the windows last night. The flat was on the second floor. His skeleton key easily opened the simple lock, and he walked in.

Asman had a living room, a bedroom, a bathroom, and a tiny kitchen. Kennelly guessed that he rented the place furnished, since all the furniture was obviously worn beyond the use he could have given it in the year or so he had lived there.

A three-cushion davenport was upholstered in mulberry velour; a matching wing chair sat on rockers. Gold braid and a chenille flower decorated the shade on a wrought-iron floor lamp. A cathedral radio sat on a heavy, ornate, yellow-oak table, and beside it sat a portable phonograph. Records were stacked on the shelf beneath. The big glass ashtray on the smoking stand was filled with the butts of the little cigars Asman favored—together with a few cigarette butts Kennelly guessed were Stormy Skye's.

The kitchen was furnished with a porcelain-top table and two chairs, plus a kitchen cabinet containing a huge flower bin with a sifter, a sugar dispenser, and storage drawers for bread and other food. There was a sink and a two-burner electric hot plate but no ice box or refrigerator. A percolator sat on the hot plate. Cups and saucers were in the sink. Asman had breakfasts of toast and coffee there, from the look of the kitchen—and ate all his other meals out.

The bedroom was furnished with an iron double bed, a dresser, and an oak rocking chair.

The bathroom was ordinary—except that the cabinet over the basin contained lipstick, rouge, and mascara.

Kennelly sighed. The things a man had to do in this business! He went to the kitchen, got a fork from the cabinet, and in the bathroom used the utensil to pull a wad of dark hair out of the drain in the basin. Dark hair. Long dark hair. Not Stormy Skye's and not Joan Fisher's, since both of them were blonde.

He used the fork in the bathtub drain. Same thing. He put a generous sample of the wadded hair in an envelope to take with him.

Now he went through the dresser drawers.

A handsome gold watch. A *very* handsome gold watch. So why didn't Asman carry it? Kennelly opened the back and read the inscription—JWP.

A photograph. A small photograph in a small gilt frame. It was a picture of a little girl, maybe ten years old. Straight bangs hung over her forehead, almost to her eyebrows, and she wore a big bow in her hair. She was staring at the camera with— He disliked making such a judgment, but she was staring at the camera with a stupid look, as though the photographer had surprised her, or as if she were a little afraid of the camera.

Kennelly turned the frame over. He saw nothing, but then pulled the cardboard down to get a look at the back of the photo itself. There was a stamp on it. It read:

WAGNER ART SHOP
Parma, Ohio

"Very well," said Mrs. Roosevelt. "Parma is a suburb of Cleveland. So what is proved, Lieutenant?"

"Coincidence on top of coincidence on top of coincidence," said Stan Szczygiel. "A Cleveland connection."

"The little girl could be a niece, the daughter of a friend . . ." said Mrs. Roosevelt.

"And the only photograph in his flat," said Kennelly. "In a nice frame. The only photograph he has."

"And an expensive gold watch he elects not to carry," said Szczygiel. "A watch inscribed JWP. There is more to Mr. Christian Asman than meets the eye."

"The initials . . ." said Mrs. Roosevelt. "His maternal grandfather?"

"When he applied for a job here, he listed his maternal grandparents' name as Miller."

"Then you have examined his personnel file," said the First Lady.

"Yes," said Szczygiel. "In fact, I have it here."

Mrs. Roosevelt glanced over the sheets that constituted the file for Christian Asman. He was, it said, a native of New York City, a graduate of Harvard College and Harvard Law. He had practiced law in two New York firms, and had a letter of recommendation from each of them. On one of these letters, Rexford Tugwell had written, "I know this guy Merrill" (meaning the lawyer who had written the letter). "A stuffy, self-satisfied Harvardian. I wouldn't want *him* on the staff, but his recommendation is probably meaningful." Harry Hopkins had written a report on Asman after he had worked in the White House six months. "Industrious, insightful. Distant, secretive," it read. "On balance, first class—but check with me before promoting."

"Nothing terribly significant," said Mrs. Roosevelt.

"Cleveland, Cleveland . . ." mused Szczygiel. "Cleveland keeps coming up."

"In that connection," said the First Lady, "let us not forget that Miss Dempsey is also from Cleveland—that is, from Rocky River, another suburb. A young woman strong-willed enough to graduate from Harvard Law—I mean as a woman—and to obtain a job in the White House is a formidable personality. I would agree that she is not strong enough physically to have murdered Mr. Djaković with a knife; but she might well be strong enough of will and purpose to have obtained someone to do it for her—if she had a motive to want the man dead."

"Motive," said Szczygiel. "Asman *or* Miss Dempsey. What motive?"

"Well," said Mrs. Roosevelt. "Think of blackmail. Mr. 'Shondor Jack' Djaković was—as we may say—living by his wits. What do you suppose he might have known about Mr. Asman or about Miss Dempsey—"

"Dear lady!" Szczygiel interrupted. "You have suggested we are piling coincidence on coincidence, reaching beyond the realm of reason to find a suspect. This suggestion—"

"Is based on no facts whatever," she said. "So, can we find facts?"

Kennelly spoke. "I think what I found in Asman's rooms are facts—and suggestive facts," he said. "The picture of the little girl. The watch. They suggest Asman has—or had—another life, somewhere, at some time."

"I should be most reluctant to suggest you search Miss Dempsey's lodgings," said Mrs. Roosevelt. "The intrusion distresses me. But—"

"I was tempted to ask her to come with us," said Szczygiel as he parked the unmarked black Ford half a block from the boarding house where Margaret Dempsey lived.

"Don't, for God's sake, ever suggest anything like that," said Kennelly. "She *will* come. She's got a lot of . . . spunk. Too damn much, in fact, to tell the truth."

Here they could not enter without encountering the landlady. Mrs. Finch was a spare woman, looking much like the farm housewife in *American Gothic*. She looked skeptically at Kennelly's badge and then led them into a parlor with a stark, grim character that precisely matched her own.

"I'd like for you to look at another set of credentials," said Kennelly. "Mr. Szczygiel is an agent of the United States Secret Service."

Mrs. Finch did not take their word for it. She lifted her chin so she could read Szczygiel's identification card through the bottom of her bifocals.

"I run a respectable boarding house," she said thinly.

"No suggestion of anything to the contrary," said Kennelly. "On the other hand, we've got to test your ability to keep a secret."

"I can do that as well as the next person," she said loftily.

"Not good enough," said Kennelly. "*Better* than the next person."

Mrs. Finch shrugged. "I guess I know how to keep my mouth shut. You can't run a boarding house without you can."

"All right," said Kennelly. "We want to look at the room occupied by one of your boarders. It's a routine investigation. We don't think she's done anything wrong. It's a matter of checking out a hunch. We figure the hunch is bad, but we have to know."

"You want to see Margaret's room," said Mrs. Finch. "Margaret Dempsey."

"What makes you think so?" asked Kennelly.

"She's the only one here that works at the White House," said Mrs. Finch.

"And as Lieutenant Kennelly told you," said Szczygiel, "this is one hundred per cent routine. Miss Dempsey is suspected of nothing. On the other hand, you are to regard this visit as absolutely confidential."

Mrs. Finch shrugged scornfully.

"I believe you have some problems with fire and sanitary regulations," said Kennelly grimly. "I checked into that before we came. If you speak a word to anyone, especially to Miss Dempsey, those problems are suddenly going to become very serious. Very, very serious. Do we understand each other?"

"An honest woman doesn't have a chance, running a little business," grumbled Mrs. Finch.

"Right," said Kennelly. "Not the chance of a snowball in hell."

As Kennelly and Szczygiel trudged up the stairs, carrying the key Mrs. Finch had handed them, Szczygiel said, "I'm glad Mrs. R. is not with us."

"So am I," said Kennelly.

Twice in one day, was his thought.

Margaret Dempsey occupied a large sunny bedroom with a bath on the second floor, overlooking the street. Searching around, with a pronounced sense of intrusion, the two officers at first saw nothing that appeared in the least out of the ordinary.

It was their duty, though, to compound the intrusion itself with a thorough examination of Margaret's quarters. Szczygiel, for one, hoped they would find nothing.

Kennelly always felt like a voyeur when he rummaged through a woman's dresser, examining her most intimate things.

Szczygiel, however, stood back, actually unwilling to do it, so Kennelly went quickly through Margaret's clothes. The top drawers of the dresser contained a few personal items—a letter from a dentist reminding her to pay her bill, several newspaper clippings from Cleveland papers announcing her appointments in Washington, a bank book, a few handwritten letters.

The letters. From her father. Kennelly pulled them from the envelopes one by one and scanned them quickly.

Her father, from the tenor of the letters, was a lawyer, practicing in downtown Cleveland. He wrote in an old-fashioned, spidery, Spencerian hand, in dark-green ink.

"Stan . . . Let me read you something," said Kennelly. "'I think you could return to Cleveland and practice law here. Although our firm would not, of course, take you in, we having no female lawyers on our staff and a determination among the partners that no woman shall ever be accepted here. You could, though, open an office of your own or join some other young lawyer in partnership, perhaps in Rocky River, and I am sure you would obtain business and do well. I will, of course, take care of your expenses until your fees meet them. The old scandal, if that is what it should be called, is rapidly being forgotten. I think you would find no prejudice against you, and in fact you would quickly discover that you have many sympathetic friends here. Think it over. Your mother and I would be so pleased to have our darling girl near home.'"

"I suppose we'll have to find out," said Szczygiel glumly.

Kennelly tucked the letter back into its envelope. "We'll have to find out," he agreed. "What the 'old scandal' was."

"'Old scandal,'" Szczygiel repeated. "Prejudice against her. She has sympathetic friends." He shook his head. "I have this awful sense we may be about to revive something that had better be left buried."

"That's what criminal investigation does sometimes," said Kennelly. "Let me look in this— My God!"

"Now what?"

Kennelly was staring at the bank book. "Monongahela Bank, Pittsburgh," he said. "On July seventeen, nineteen thirty, Margaret Dempsey deposited ten thousand dollars in a savings account. She's never drawn on it. The money has been lying there accumulating interest for seven years, almost. She's got over thirteen thousand dollars. That's three . . . four year's income for a White House lawyer. More than."

Stan Szczygiel threw out his hands. "Her father says he'd pay her expenses until she got herself established in the law in Cleveland. Hell, he wouldn't have to. Which means—"

"Which means," said Kennelly, "that her father doesn't know about Margaret's thirteen thou."

"Not necessarily," said Mrs. Roosevelt.

Szczygiel grinned. "Ma'am," he said, "I wish I had a nickel for every time I've heard you say 'not necessarily.'"

She was once again distracted. Newspaper reaction to the court-reform plan, which was being called "the court-packing" plan, had already begun to come in. Not one story, not one editorial, was positive. The afternoon papers were attacking with vigor.

What was perhaps worse, they were quoting leaders in Congress, who were calling the plan unconstitutional at best, and things like "an arbitrary, high-handed, arrogant power-grab" at worst. The First Lady had to wonder, almost, if Franklin's sure instinct for the political climate of the nation had not for once failed him.

"We have to know what the scandal in Cleveland was," said Szczygiel.

"I shall find out," said the First Lady. "I have newspaper friends there who can look into it for me."

"I've something else to show you," said Kennelly. He withdrew from the inside pocket of his jacket an envelope bulging with a wad of dark hair. "She has her own bathroom. I find myself digging hair out of people's drains lately. This—"

"Does not necessarily match that which you found in Mr. Asman's drains," said Mrs. Roosevelt.

The President, too, read the newspapers that afternoon. He shrugged, stiffened his jaw, and told Harry Hopkins that the court-reform bill would pass, no matter what. On this one, he would not back down.

Anyway, he was looking forward to the evening. Harry Hopkins, as head of WPA, had sponsored the Federal Theater Project; and, with help from the President and Mrs. Roosevelt, had obtained modest funding for the project by Congress. The idea had been to provide jobs for unemployed theater people, not just performers but everyone from playwrights to prop men. FTP had been a significant, though highly controversial, success. Tonight, a group of its beneficiaries were holding a dinner for the chief benefactors.

Unfortunately, the First Lady had been long committed to a dinner of the NAACP. She was sending her greetings and would not be present for the FTP gala, which was being held in a theater on the campus of Georgetown University.

Even so, the President could not have been more enthusiastic. With Hopkins, he left the White House at seven that evening as snow began to fall. The President wore a top hat and his heavy wool naval cape.

Ranks of tables had been set up toward the rear of the big stage, leaving room for small performances at the front. Hundreds of guests would eat their dinners from trays balanced on their laps in their theater seats.

No one would make a speech tonight. Not even the President. After the dinner, small groups of actors would perform scenes from plays staged by the FTP. So far as the President was concerned, it would be a perfect evening.

During the cocktail hour, the President was to be seated at a table in the center of the stage, and guests were welcome to come forward to shake his hand and greet him. Many of the guests had never participated in an FTP production. They were simply theater-oriented people who appreciated the project and wanted to honor it and its sponsors.

The President was filled with joy as he was welcomed by Lee J. Cobb, Elia Kazan, Karl Malden, Clifton Webb, Fred Allen, Walter Huston, George Murphy, Bob Hope, Ethel Walters, and Fred Astaire.

"Are you going to dance for us, Fred?" he asked Astaire.

"Why, yes, Mr. President. Certainly."

"Well, I'm sorry I can't join you for a duo."

Astaire blushed deep red, but the President, who held Astaire's hand in a firm grip, drew him closer and closed his own left hand over the dancer's right, making the handshake more friendly and intimate. The President's laugh was so genuine and hearty that in a moment Fred Astaire was laughing too.

Some playwrights were there, as well, and the President greeted Clifford Odets, George S. Kaufman, and Moss Hart.

At eight-thirty, Hallie Flanagan, head of the Federal Theater Project, escorted the President and Harry Hopkins to their places at the highest table. No blessing was pronounced, no one was introduced. The dinner was served.

Seated beside the President was one of the most active participants in the FTP, the talented young actor Orson Welles. Seated by Hopkins was another noted FTP actor, John Houseman.

"You are a controversial young man, Mr. Welles," the President said cheerfully.

Welles was that. He was also fervent. Two years ago, only twenty, he had created a radio sensation in the role of Lamont Cranston, "The Shadow." ("Who *knows* what *evil* . . . lurks in the hearts of men? The Shadow knows.") One year ago he had staged an all-Negro FTP production of *Macbeth*—all Negro, that is, except that Welles himself played the title character. He had set his *Macbeth* not in Scotland but in Haiti, under its black emperor, Henri Christophe. The production had been hailed as a work of unparalleled genius.

More recently Welles and Houseman had created high

controversy by staging Mark Blitzstein's *The Cradle Will Rock*, a scathing, satirical condemnation of labor conditions in the steel industry. This had proved too much for the FTP administrators, and they had withdrawn their support. Welles and Houseman were going ahead independently.

Welles looked like the youth he was, with his dark hair combed from left to right, somber eyes, and a lower lip habitually thrust forward in the beginning of a pout. The President noticed also that the young man's flesh was not quite firm enough for a boy his age, suggesting that Welles was going to be a fat man if he wasn't careful.

"Mr. President," said Welles solemnly, "I am not altogether certain that federal funding of theater is entirely a good idea."

"He who pays the piper calls the tune," said the President.

"Exactly. A lot of theater people have been put back to work, and I'm glad of that, but I'm not sure the FTP should be continued after the economic crisis is over."

"You're afraid of censorship, then?"

"I am, Sir. We've experienced it already. With whatever good intentions the Congress appropriates money for theater, it is bound, sooner or later, to want to have some say in what kind of plays are staged. So . . . plays with social commentary in them—"

"Will be denied funding," the President finished the sentence.

"Precisely," said Welles.

"You are not a politician," said the President. "And you shouldn't be. Politics is the craft of compromise; and in the arts, compromise is the source of ruin."

"I might hope, Mr. President, you would see fit to

speak out, at some appropriate time, against censorship."

"Well—"

Hopkins, who had heard their discussion, spoke past Hallie Flanagan and said, "Houseman here has something to say about censorship."

The President smiled. "Let us hear it."

John Houseman leaned forward so he could speak directly to the President. "Are you aware, Mr. President, that the Clifford Odets play *Waiting for Lefty*—which is a condemnation of anti-Semitism—can't be staged in Boston? They call it obscene."

The President laughed. "In Boston, *Alice in Wonderland* is obscene."

"They call it blasphemous," Houseman added. "And have prosecuted. Except in Boston, nobody has been prosecuted for blasphemy since the Middle Ages."

"Except in Massachusetts," said Welles angrily, "no one has been burned as a witch since the Middle Ages."

"When I was at Harvard," said the President, "we used to sneak into Boston and go to the old . . . What was it called? The Howard Theater? I could be wrong. The notorious Boston burlesque house. But none of the young ladies was burned as a witch, that I recall."

"Stripteasers don't express ideas, Mr. President," said Houseman. "That's what they can't stand in Boston. Ideas."

"I believe I did notice that," said the President. "Boston has that in common with a lot of cities, if we are to believe their newspapers."

Mrs. Roosevelt returned to the White House before the President. She sat down at her desk, and after pondering for a long moment she placed a long-distance telephone call to Cleveland.

"Harriet?" she said when the call was completed and a woman's voice came on the line. "This is Eleanor. Eleanor. Calling from the White House. I wonder if I might ask you a favor."

Harriet was the wife of a newspaper publisher. She and the First Lady had been friends for many years.

"A confidential matter, Harriet, if you don't mind. It may mean nothing at all, but I would be grateful if you could check your newspaper morgue files and see if they contain some information."

The woman said she would be glad to.

"Very well. We have working in the White House a really outstanding young woman, for whom I have great respect. She is a lawyer. There is some suggestion that she was involved in a scandal in Cleveland. A public scandal perhaps. Could you check into it for me? Her name is Margaret Dempsey."

6

They were not very happy with the work, but Stan Szczygiel and Ed Kennelly spent that evening tailing Margaret Dempsey and Christian Asman—both of them—as wet snow continued to fall over Washington.

The young woman was easy. She left the White House a little after six, sat alone over dinner with wine at Harvey's and took a cab home. There was no point, the men judged, in sitting outside her boarding house for hours, so they moved on to the Farragut Bar to look for Asman.

He was not there. Kennelly drove to his apartment building. The lights were on. Apparently he was home. They watched for an hour, smoking cigarettes and talking. Then he came out. But not alone. Joan Fisher, the senator's daughter, was with him. He had telephoned for a cab, evidently, since one came around the corner and picked him up within minutes. He took Joan Fisher home to Georgetown, then had the cab drop him at the Farragut.

Within twenty minutes of sitting down at a table in the bar, he was joined by a young woman, this one a redhead. Immediately they were more than friendly.

The redhead was svelte. Her tight green dress complemented her flaming red hair, which hung unstylishly long, over her shoulders. If there was a flaw to her face and figure, neither Kennelly or Szczygiel could identify it.

"I'm damned," said Kennelly, "if I understand the attraction. He don't look handsome to me."

"If we understood the attraction, Kennelly, we could do it ourselves," said Szczygiel wryly.

"You've gotta figure," said Kennelly, "that the Fisher girl is respectable—anyway, is respectable if you can use the word about a girl who's just spent a couple hours in Asman's flat. I wonder—"

"You wonder what the senator thinks," said Szczygiel. "Let me fill you in a little. Joan Fisher is twenty-seven. Her father is in his third term in the Senate, so she's lived in Washington mostly for the last fifteen years or so. Her mother is a semi-invalid. The girl helps take care of the old lady. She knows her way around in Washington. I mean, knows her way around. She did the cocktail parties when cocktail parties were illegal. She was engaged to a Republican congressman from Ohio, but it fell apart for some reason. What's her father know? No way to tell. I'd guess he doesn't watch her too closely."

"A modern girl," said Kennelly.

"Figure it out."

The redhead was maybe the most attractive of the girls they had seen Asman with. He was attentive to her, as he had been to Joan Fisher and Stormy Skye, and she seemed to love it.

He smoked one of his little cigars, just the same, and as always let the stream of smoke rise up behind his eyeglasses and into his sandy hair. He had a way of smiling that disgusted Szczygiel: upturning the corners of his wide, thin lips while keeping his mouth closed and his teeth hidden. He leaned toward the redhead and spoke to her in what looked like—undoubtedly was meant to look like—conspiratorial confidentiality, as if he were giving her secrets from the White House.

And maybe that was, in fact, what he was doing—telling her secrets he was making up as he went along, to impress her.

Whatever he was doing, she seemed to like it. She smoked a cigarette, sipped whiskey, and giggled.

Kennelly had turned sullenly impatient. He summoned the bartender, showed him his badge, and asked, "Who's the redhead?"

The bartender shrugged. "Dunno," he said.

"Hooker?"

"Could be, but I don't think so."

"Come in a lot?"

The bartender shook his head. "Occasionally," he said. "Ask Millie. I see them talkin' once in a while."

"Millie . . . ?"

The bartender nodded toward one of the waitresses and at the same time beckoned her to come to the bar. He spoke to her very quietly, so that others at the bar would not hear. "Talk to this guy," he said. "He's a cop."

The waitress was a brunette, but she had bleached her hair the color of straw. It was tightly curled and looked just as brittle. Her bright-red lipstick was carelessly smeared across her mouth. She wore a white yachting cap, a shiny, over-laundered and overstarched white jacket, and a tiny blue skirt that covered her hips and not much below, leaving her legs bare.

Kennelly showed her his badge. "Who's the redhead?" he asked.

"Teddy O'Neil," said the waitress. "Theodora's her name, actually. Theodora O'Neil."

"Who is she?" Kennelly asked.

Millie glanced at the redhead. "Well . . . she's, uh, what you might call a professional girl."

"A hooker."

"I don't think I'd call her that. She's very professional, very high-priced, very discreet. I mean, like, that guy there, he can't pick her up. She don't work that way."

"He seems to know her," said Kennelly.

"Well, he does. He knows her. But she won't leave here with him. She won't leave here with any guy. They have to make their arrangements by phone."

"How do you come to know her?"

The waitress flared with temper. "I s'pose you've gotta know—you being a cop," she complained.

Kennelly smiled and nodded. "Right. I've gotta know."

She sighed noisily. "Okay, if you've gotta know. I tried to do what she does myself. Only I couldn't work it like she does."

"How does she work it?"

"You've gotta call her number. Some gal answers. You make an appointment."

"Why couldn't you do that?"

Millie turned down the corners of her mouth. "You've gotta have a place with a phone," she said. "You've gotta have somebody workin' for ya, to take your calls. And you've gotta be—Well, look at her," she concluded with sullen jealousy.

"You don't happen to have that phone number or know where she lives?"

Millie shook her head.

"Okay, what about the guy with her? Who's he?"

"I don't know. He comes in here a lot." She shrugged. "Maybe she works for him. Maybe some other girls do. He meets a blonde here. I don't know who she is. Also an older woman. I don't know who she is either."

When Millie had gone back to carrying drinks, Szczygiel spoke to Kennelly and said, "Why do I get the idea that all we're doing is studying a guy's love life? What's the connection?"

"Shondor Jack was from Cleveland," said Kennelly. "Margaret Dempsey is from Cleveland. Stormy Skye spent some time in Cleveland. I'm going to find out if Teddy O'Neil is from Cleveland."

"But Chris Asman is from New York."

"So he says."

"His letters of recommendation, from some respectable New York lawyers, say he's from New York."

"Look," said Kennelly. "None of these girls killed Shondor Jack. None of them have got the muscle power that took. Anyway, we know damned well that neither Stormy Skye nor Teddy O'Neil was in the White House Wednesday night. They could hardly get in and not be noticed. Joan Fisher could probably walk in. With her style, she wouldn't be conspicuous. But do you think that little blonde killed Shondor? The killer was a man, and the only man we know was near the Red Room and didn't have any business there is Asman. Besides, he's the only suspect we've got."

"I wish we had another one," said Szczygiel glumly.

"Well . . . How'd you like to talk to Stormy Skye?"

Szczygiel rubbed his stomach. "I haven't done this much barhopping since before Prohibition."

"We won't see her at the Gayety Bar. I'll call headquarters and have her picked up after the show. We'll question her in my office."

Stan Szczygiel had been in Ed Kennelly's office before and had often wondered why no one—Ed himself or somebody in charge of cleaning—couldn't sweep the dead flies off the window sill. After all, this was February, which meant those flies had been there since October, if not before—if in fact they hadn't been accumulating since 1932.

He had seldom drunk worse coffee, but he said he'd accept a cup just the same. Ed washed out two mugs in the basin beside his desk and stepped into the hall to pour coffee from the two-gallon blue ironware pot that steamed on a hot plate.

Only when their cups of coffee were in their hands did Kennelly send a uniformed matron to bring in Stormy Skye.

"What the hell is this?" she demanded angrily as she came through the door. "What you harrassin' me for? My show has been cleared by—"

"Sit down, Gerty," said Kennelly. "And don't get smart-aleck with me. I've got a few easy questions for you. Answer them, you can leave."

The tall striptease dancer glanced at Szczygiel, looked around the littered, dusty office, then sat down on the wooden straight chair that was the only seat left. She had been arrested before she left the theater, and she still wore her stage makeup. Seeing her close now, in the light, Szczygiel realized that Stormy Skye was a little shopworn. The flesh around her jaw sagged. She had a scar on her left cheek, just under her eye. She had a voluptuous figure, though—assuming that was what they called it—and he resolved to slip into the Gayety Theater before her run there ended and see some more of it. Her red dress was stretched tight over her flesh. It might have been more glamorous if the armpits had not been stained with sweat.

"Gertrude Schmidt," said Kennelly. "From Elkins, West Virginia. A coal miner's daughter, I bet."

"Damn right," she muttered.

"I bet he beat your ass when he found out what you were."

Her chin jerked up, and then she nodded and repeated, "Damn right."

Kennelly grinned. "Spent some time in jail in Cleveland," he said.

"I was a victim of prejudice," she said.

"Sure. Okay, Gerty. When did you last see Shondor Jack?"

She shook her head. "I don't know anybody by that name."

"Gerty—Aleksandr Djaković. When did you last see him?"

"I never heard of the guy!"

"'Kay. That's not what we call cooperation. I guess we're going to have to keep you here a while—till we see if your memory improves."

Kennelly lurched out from behind his desk and strode into the hall. "Beth! You can take Miss Schmidt back and lock her up. I won't need her any more tonight."

"Hey! Wait a minute!" the stripteaser yelled as the

matron appeared in the doorway. "Hey! What was that name again?"

"Shondor Jack," said Kennelly. "Aleksandr Djaković."

She glanced fearfully over her shoulder at the police matron. "Shondor . . ." she muttered. "Well. Yeah, I've heard the name."

"Keep talkin'."

"Well, he— He was a crook. In Cleveland. He, uh . . . He made girls work for him. You know what I mean?"

"I know what you mean."

"He was a small-timer, a cheap little crook with ambitions to be a big crook. He spent a lot of time in the pen. But his sentences would run out, and he'd come back to Cleveland. The cops in Cleveland really had it in for him. They were going to get him one way or another. He beat a lot of raps. Maybe because they were too anxious. Then they got him. I mean, they got him for sure."

"Meaning . . . ?"

"Well it was—let's see—nineteen-thirty. Yeah, nineteen-thirty. They got him for Murder One, the big one. But he beat that rap. He had an alibi witness, a little girl everybody had to believe. But he wasn't out two weeks before they grabbed him again on a burglary rap. And that one they made stick. Which made three convictions for burglary—which made him what they call a habitual criminal. They dropped an indictment on him for being a habitual criminal. The conviction was automatic. He got a life sentence."

"But he didn't serve any of it," said Szczygiel.

"No, he escaped. But girls like me were glad to see him gone from Cleveland. Whenever he was down at the heels, he'd recruit two or three girls. Beat 'em if they didn't wanta work for him. I'll be damned glad to see that son of a bitch get his."

"Really? Then I suppose you are extra happy now."

"What ya talkin' about?"

"Why you're here," said Kennelly. "The son of a bitch got his."

"Mystery to me, buddy," said Stormy Skye.

Kennelly lifted his mug and took a big swallow of coffee. Szczygiel had noticed that the detective had not offered the woman any coffee. He called her by her first name. He treated her like a naughty child, only tougher. It was a technique of restrained interrogation he had learned over the years: a crude method favored by police officers, which didn't work with halfway sophisticated subjects.

"Gerty . . . Why you figure you're here?"

She shook her head. "I've got no idea," she said, and Szczygiel was satisfied she really didn't.

"Remember the question I asked you a while ago?" Kennelly asked her.

"Which was?"

"When did you last see Shondor Jack?"

She stared at him for a long moment. "Uh . . . God . . . What? Say six or seven years ago?"

"You know where he is now?" Kennelly asked.

She shook her head.

"Shondor Jack," said Kennelly, "lies in the morgue. Here in Washington. Murdered Wednesday night. Now, you wanta start over on the question of when you last saw him?"

The shopworn stripteaser could show shock and fear, even through the heavy stage makeup on her face. "No . . ." She said, and she began to shake her head.

"What? Wednesday night? What time? I was on the goddam stage three times Wednesday night, damn near naked. Seen by hundreds. What time?"

"Would you like a cup of coffee, Gert?" Kennelly asked. He rose and rinsed out another mug and handed it to the matron, who still waited in the doorway. "We know you didn't kill him. But we figure you know things that may help us find out who did." He leaned back in his chair and grinned at her. "Okay, kid," he said. "What can you tell us? We've got no Murder One on you, but it's a Murder One investigation, so you know we're not fooling around."

"I saw him Sunday," she said.

Saturday morning was ordinarily a slow time at the White House, as it was everywhere: a relaxed time when people read documents they had put aside during the hectic weekdays and returned telephone calls they had not gotten around to making earlier.

Saturday morning, February 6, 1937, however, was hectic at the White House. The press was attacking. The afternoon papers yesterday had been bad enough. The Saturday morning papers were worse.

The *New York Herald Tribune*: "[This proposal] would end the American state as it has existed throughout the long years of its life."

The *Boston Herald*: "It is not a judicial readjustment which he seeks but an enlargement of his own powers."

What the editorials talked about was the Constitution. About the American tradition. About patriotism. They waved the shirts of George Washington, Thomas Jefferson, Andrew Jackson, and Woodrow Wilson—not to mention the Republicans Abraham Lincoln and Theodore Roosevelt. The Supreme Court was a respected institution. The President knew that. Suddenly it was sanctified.

He cared little about editorials. The nation's press would have elected Alf Landon, if it could have. It would have blocked his nomination in 1932, if it could have. It had condemned the New Deal with near unanimity. He had always said no one was for him but the people.

But . . . Senator Ed Burke of Nebraska was quoted as saying, "I love the President. I think he has done wonderful things. I admire him, but not on this court proposal."

One paper reported—and who could doubt it was true?—that Vice President Garner, though he would keep silent, was privately "disgusted" by the court-reform bill.

Coming from last night's happy dinner for the Federal Theater Project, the President was shocked to read about his disintegrating support. Unless the newspapers were lying, he was losing the backing of congressional leaders he had counted on in this crucial fight.

Well—Only one thing to do. By God, he would fight!

The President sat up in bed, reading newspapers and irritably tossing them to the floor. Missy, still in her nightgown and peignoir, sat at the foot of the bed, catching them in turn, so she could look at them herself.

"One . . . good . . . point," the President muttered. "I've been roundly condemned by the Daughters of the American Revolution. The lunatic fringe has weighed in. That ought to count for something in winning some support from the rational. I'm a Dutchman, you know, Missy. That puts a strain of stubbornness in me. I'm going forward with this thing. To the end. Win or lose. A man who hasn't got the guts to do that—"

"Boss . . . Everyone who cares for you is with you," said Missy tearfully. The evil things said about him in the newspapers had never gone past her without bringing tears. "You don't have to ask who's with you. Do you?"

He put his right hand on her cheek. "No," he said. "Never a doubt. Never for a minute."

Mrs. Roosevelt would, of course, support the President, without qualification—but she wasn't sure how. She had always looked for ways to support Franklin in everything he did, even when—as was sometimes the case—he did not ask for her help or suggest how she might give it. And even when she did not entirely agree with him.

Experience suggested that he would know he had her loyalty and that it would be pointless to go to his bedroom and tell him so. She left her own bedroom early and went downstairs to the Private Dining Room, where she had a long-standing appointment to take breakfast with Mary McLeod Bethune.

She spent a pleasant hour with the woman who was fighting quietly but effectively for the improvement of her race. "In the South our people can't vote," said Mrs. Bethune. "In the North we can and do. But only for candidates that other people nominate. Negroes are effectively shut out of the political *process*."

The First Lady had that statement in mind later as she hurried upstairs to her office, where Agent Szczygiel and Lieutenant Kennelly were waiting.

Ed Kennelly had been chatting with Stan Szczygiel and staring once again around the First Lady's office. He had been there a good many times before, but he never ceased to be intrigued by the fact that he, an Irish cop and son of an Irish cop, should have become familiar with a private office on the second floor of the White House.

The room was modestly furnished. Mrs. Roosevelt's desk was small, and it was not—if he were any judge—a real antique. To her left on the desktop sat a stack of three letter boxes. To her right stood a Dictaphone. A couple of extra recording cylinders lay in front of the machine. She sat on a simple wooden armchair with a woven seat and a thin cushion pad, positioned on the bare floor. Framed photographs—family mostly, though one was of Louis McHenry Howe—decorated the walls. On a cabinet to one side of her desk sat a model of a sailing ship. Other chairs rested on a somewhat worn Oriental rug.

"Progress, gentlemen?" she asked as she hurried in. "I'm sorry that my schedule has kept me rather fully occupied."

"We've made progress," said Kennelly with measured enthusiasm.

Mrs. Roosevelt listened and nodded, but she frowned hard over a telephone note left on her desk. "Uh . . . Excuse me for a moment, please," she said. "I seem to have an urgent call. At least it's an emphatic demand that I call Harry Hopkins immediately. I doubt it will take more than a moment."

She told the White House operator to put her through to Hopkins. He was in his office in the West Wing.

"Harry—"

"Oh. Thanks for being quick, Eleanor," said Hopkins

briskly through the wire. "Are you still taking an interest in that murder in the Red Room?"

"Definitely," she said.

"Is that lawyer who works for me still a suspect? Asman?"

"It's not terribly serious, Harry. We really have no evidence against him."

"Well, I have something against him," said Hopkins crisply. "It may be more comic than serious. I had a call this morning from Senator John Fisher. He complains that Asman is, as he puts it, 'trying to ruin my little girl,' and he wants me to order Asman to stay away from his daughter."

"Oh, dear."

"He's an outraged father, let me tell you. I had to say I'd give Asman the word. He sounded as if he might be coming over here with a pistol—at least with a bull whip—if I didn't."

"Have you spoken to Mr. Asman?"

"I thought I'd check with you first."

"Well, do talk to him, Harry," she said. "I'd like to know how he reacts."

She turned to Szczygiel and Kennelly. "Do you have anything further on Mr. Asman?"

"He spent some time in his apartment with Joan Fisher last evening," said Szczygiel. "Then he went to the Farragut Bar and spent some time in close conversation with a high-priced prostitute."

"Oh, *dear*."

"Let us tell you what else we found out last night," said Kennelly. "We questioned the stripper. It turns out that she knew Shondor Jack, as we suspected. She hated him. She would have liked to kill him. But she couldn't have."

"On the other hand," said Szczygiel, "maybe she somehow procured someone to do it for her. She becomes another suspect anyway."

"It is not, I suppose, impossible," said Mrs. Roosevelt, "that she procured Mr. Asman to do it for her. In which case, we do not have another suspect."

"She had motive," said Kennelly. "Djaković abused her in Cleveland, forced her to hand over her earnings as a prostitute. Then here in Washington, as recently as Sunday, he tried to extort money from her."

"He threatened to cut her," said Stan Szczygiel. "To scar her face and body so she couldn't work on the stage anymore."

"Ohh . . ." murmured Mrs. Roosevelt.

"He was running some prostitutes here in Washington," said Kennelly. "That's how he lived. A fugitive from a life sentence. For six-and-a-half years."

"Well . . ." said the First Lady, shaking her head. "I—"

She was interrupted by the telephone. It was Hopkins.

"You wanted to know how Asman reacts. Okay. He reacts by saying he hopes he hasn't caused any embarrassment and he won't see the girl again."

"Did he not protest?"

"No. He took the word very calmly. Didn't even blink. Said something to the effect that Joan Fisher is old enough to choose her own company but that he didn't want to cause a fuss."

Mrs. Roosevelt picked up the yellow pad on which she had been writing notes about the case. She flipped to a new page. "It's all questions," she said. "I'd like to have an answer to just one of them." Then she wrote some new questions:

Is Miss Skye really a suspect?
Could she have procured the murder?
What, exactly, is Mr. Asman's relationship to Miss Skye?
What is Mr. Asman's relationship to the prostitute in the bar?
Are we focusing too much on Mr. Asman?

"I am particularly concerned with the last question," she said. "We have focused our attention almost exclusively on this one person. I know it's because he's the only suspect we have, but I believe we should be rethinking the case. Others had motive to murder Mr. Djaković."

"In the White House?" asked Szczygiel.

Mrs. Roosevelt frowned and sighed. "How did he get in here? And why? We *must* find out."

"You have to accept one fact, Ma'am," said Kennelly.

"Which is?"

"That some murders are never solved. We may never find out how Shondor Jack got into the White House. We may never find out who killed him. I have lots of open files at headquarters. Some of them have been open for many years."

Standing at the window of her office an hour after Szczygiel and Kennelly left, the First Lady looked out across the Ellipse, where green patches showed through the melting snow. She stared for a moment at the Washington Monument.

She had spent time with her correspondence, scribbling notes on letters, so Tommy could type the answers Monday. She had dictated two of her newspaper columns onto the black cylinder in the Dictaphone. The letter boxes remained full, even so. Sometimes it seemed there was no end of correspondence.

It was understandable, yet strange, how simple people thought the President or the First Lady could solve any problem. They wrote about missing children, whom they were sure people as powerful as the President and his wife could find. They wrote about wells gone dry. About sick pigs. About frozen pipes. About sullen schoolteachers. About bad dreams. About heart attacks. About visitations by spirits. About the wind blowing away the soil from the fields.

Many of the letters she could not answer. Others were answered by Tommy:

> Dear Mrs. Jones,
>
> Mrs. Roosevelt has received your letter and asked me to answer for her, to say that she too has often been puzzled by the meaning of the seventeenth chapter of Revelation. She believes her interpretation is not likely to be better than your own and suggests you discuss the interpretation with your pastor.
>
> Mrs. Roosevelt has directed me to thank you for your letter.
>
> Sincerely yours,
>
> Malvina Thompson
> Secretary to Mrs. Roosevelt

The telephone rang. The operator said the call was from Cleveland, from a Mrs. Harriet Seltzer. The First Lady took the call.

"Harriet, how nice to hear from you again so soon!"

"Your question about Margaret Dempsey has produced an interesting little story," said the woman in Cleveland.

"I was afraid it might."

"Yes. Well, Margaret Dempsey is the daughter of a prominent Cleveland attorney. She is an intelligent, attractive, personable young woman, everyone says. But there is a strange quirk to her life story."

"I should be grateful to hear all about it."

"It seems she was the star witness here in Cleveland in nineteen-thirty. A notorious criminal was on trial in Common Pleas Court, on a charge of murder. His name was Aleksandr Djaković, known around here as Shondor Jack. The evidence showed he had strong motive to want to kill a certain man, another gangster by the name of Ronald Cairns. The man was found at five-thirty in the afternoon, in the trunk of an automobile parked on the lakefront. He was still alive, and obviously had been shot within the hour—that is, between, say, three forty-five and maybe five-fifteen. He died soon after he was found. Ballistics tests proved that he was killed with a gun known to belong to Shondor Jack. The police arrested Jack—Djaković—and charged him with the murder. It looked like a tight case, until his alibi witness appeared."

"Margaret Dempsey?" asked Mrs. Roosevelt.

"Yes. At the time, she was a student at Western Reserve University and was about twenty or twenty-one years old. She testified that a group of girls had decided to have a party. They wanted to serve liquor, and the problem was where to get some—Prohibition still being the law. Margaret Dempsey testified that she had volunteered to get the liquor, since she knew where to obtain it. The girls chipped in the money, and Margaret drove down to the Ninth Street pier, went in the restaurant there, and asked for Shondor Jack. He was upstairs, and he came down. She told him she wanted a case of real Scotch. He told her she'd have to come with him to Lorain, which was the closest place where he could come up with a whole case of the real stuff. They drove to Lorain in her car. It's about twenty or twenty-five miles. He directed her to a warehouse, where he sold her the Scotch, and she drove him back to the pier."

"Which took an hour or more, I suppose," said Mrs. Roosevelt.

"She testified that she met the man about two forty-five and dropped him back at the pier at five forty-five. Three hours. It would take maybe an hour to drive to Lorain, considering the streets and roads and the traffic. Then an hour to come back. But she also testified that they had stayed in the warehouse for a while, taking a couple of drinks from the Scotch. She had to know it was genuine, she said. Also, she had to fend off a proposition from Shondor Jack. Anyway, she was sure about the times: that she had picked him up very close to two forty-five and dropped him back at the pier within a few minutes of five forty-five."

"A perfect alibi," said Mrs. Roosevelt.

"The more so since the girl was young, pretty, obviously bright—and of a good family with an impeccable reputation. The bootlegger from Lorain testified, too, but his testimony meant nothing compared to hers. That young, obviously innocent, frightened girl on the witness stand . . . Well, it won the acquittal."

"Even so, the matter created a scandal, did it not?"

"Oh, yes. Shortly after his acquittal in the murder trial,

Shondor Jack was convicted of another crime and sentenced to life imprisonment. He escaped and has not been seen or heard of since. When Margaret Dempsey went off to Harvard for law school, there were those in Cleveland who said she had gone away with Shondor Jack. There are those who will never believe she didn't lie for him."

7

"I regret it, Miss Dempsey," said Mrs. Roosevelt. "I hope the matter can be kept personal and confidential. I have not even given the information to the two investigators working on the case, Mr. Szczygiel and Lieutenant Kennelly. Perhaps I won't have to."

Margaret Dempsey drew a long breath. She was a young woman who appealed to the First Lady, and the new information about her did not change that. As before, she was modestly dressed now in a yellow cardigan sweater with a string of pearls at her throat, and a dark-gray skirt.

"I was compelled to make the inquiry," said Mrs. Roosevelt, hoping Margaret would never find out that she had felt so compelled because the two investigators had invaded the young woman's room and read the personal letters they had found in her dresser drawer.

"The whole thing has been a nightmare," said Margaret Dempsey. "Starting with a decision to buy some bootleg whiskey, seven years ago."

"Did you in fact go with Mr. Djaković to Lorain to buy a case of Scotch?"

"I testified to that, Mrs. Roosevelt," said Margaret Dempsey a little coldly. "I swore to it, under oath."

"Yes, of course. And the result was that Mr. . . . uh, Jack, Mr. Shondor Jack, was acquitted."

"He was innocent," said Margaret Dempsey. "He was guilty of a great many other crimes, but he could not have murdered Ronald Cairns."

"How did you come to testify in his behalf? Did you volunteer?"

"Not long after he was arrested, his lawyer called me. He'd told the lawyer he was with me that afternoon."

"Did you ever see him after—"

"Mrs. Roosevelt, I saw Shondor Jack four times. I had bought liquor from him twice before the fatal afternoon. I was with him that day. I saw him at the trial. I have never seen him since."

"Never here in Washington?"

"Absolutely not. And let me say to you, I could be glad he is dead—except for one thing. When the story of his death reaches the newspapers, particularly in Cleveland, it will revive the old scandal. There are people who think I was his girlfriend. They, of course, think I lied under oath to save him."

Mrs. Roosevelt nodded. "I quite understand, my dear," she said. "We will do anything we can to avoid your being embarrassed."

"I will be grateful," said Margaret Dempsey.

The young woman left. The First Lady found it all but impossible to disbelieve her. Yet— She opened her desk and took out two pieces of paper: the criminal record of

Aleksandr Djaković, and the note she had made on lined yellow paper on the information Lieutenant Kennelly had taken from Miss Dempsey's bank book.

Shondor Jack's 1930 acquittal was on Tuesday, July 15. On Thursday, the seventeenth, Margaret Dempsey had deposited $10,000 in the Monongahela Bank in Pittsburgh.

Coincidence? It seemed this investigation was full of coincidences. And she didn't like this one.

The First Lady had put on her black coat and pulled her fox around her shoulders to go out in the cold wind that had begun to whip up the Potomac. Last night's snow had fallen from the trees in this morning's fair weather, but now what remained on the ground had frozen and crusted as temperatures dropped. She was in her bedroom when the call came from Harry Hopkins.

"Eleanor? Help! I'm about to be invaded."

She could not help but laugh. "Invaded, Harry?"

"By Senator Fisher. I called him back to tell him Asman had agreed to keep his distance from Joan Fisher, but that didn't satisfy him. He's on his way to the White House to make his complaint against Christian Asman. And I'm glad Asman has left."

"What could you possibly want me to do, Harry?"

"*Diplomacy!* Diplomacy, for God's sake! Stature . . . Maybe you—Eleanor, I can't ask the Boss to—"

She put her fox fur aside. "Where are we meeting with Senator Fisher?" she asked.

"Someplace that's got a lot of White House mystique," he said. "How 'bout the Blue Room?"

Half an hour later Mrs. Roosevelt walked into the oval

Blue Room on the first floor to confront the irate senator from Arkansas.

She had met the man before, she was sure, but still she was surprised by his appearance. Senator John Fisher was a heavy, solid, round man, probably fifty or fifty-five years old, wearing a thin black mustache on his fat, florid face.

"I ordered a selection of brandies," she said. It was by no means her wont to order spirits for such a meeting, but she had decided that an offering of drinkables from the pantry would be appropriate in this case. "I hope you find something to your liking, Senator."

The senator from Arkansas frowned over the silver tray and the bottles. "Well . . ." he said. "I hadn't thought— On the other hand, a taste of somethin' sociable . . ."

"Certainly," she said—though she mentally calculated the expense from the pantry of the generous drinks of brandy that Senator Fisher and Harry now poured. Thank heaven Harry had not called for oysters. "Something sociable . . ."

"Not your problem. Not your problem, my dear lady," the senator said after he had sampled the Courvoisier. "You will understand, though, that a father has an overridden' paternal obligation to save the honor of his only daughter."

The First Lady glanced at Hopkins, whose bland expression in the face of this statement was not helpful. And damn him . . . Harry didn't have to sit there like a Buddha.

"The question, Senator," she said, "is what the White House can do to help you with this problem."

"*Fire the son of* . . . Excuse me. Fire Asman. Run him out of Washin'ton."

"Senator . . . Your daughter is . . . what? . . . in her late twenties?" asked Mrs. Roosevelt.

"Twenty-seven," he said.

"Then perhaps she is old enough to choose her own company."

"Mrs. Roosevelt . . . Let me explain in as inoffensive terms as possible. Christian Asman has . . . *ruined* my little girl. I am sure you know what I mean. I can't say I would be pleased to have Joan datin' some cheap little New York shyster. But datin' her is one thing, and what he did to her is another."

Hopkins tried to interject a word. "Senator, I—"

"He didn't date her," the senator went on. "He didn't come to the house and pick her up, let her parents see the young man who was datin' their daughter. He met her in *bars*. He took her to his apartment, and I don't need to tell you what they did there. Not only that. They've been *seen!* I mean, she's been seen with him, sneakin' out of bars, holdin' his hand, when they have never been seen together at concerts, plays, parties, among respectable people—the kind of thing a man would do if he took a girl out of an evenin' with honorable intentions."

"What are you asking us to do, Senator?" asked the First Lady. "Discharge the young man from his employment?"

"I think that would be the right thing."

Harry Hopkins shook his head. "If we did that, Senator, it would be a political matter, out of respect for you. You speak of doing what's right. What's right is that you don't deprive a man of employment because he has engaged in a meretricious relationship with a young lady who is well past the age of consent."

Senator Fisher turned down the corners of his mouth as he lifted his chin high. "That may be, as you do things in the No'th," he said scornfully. "In the South, not only do we regard such conduct as deservin' a small thing like losin' a job. We think it deserves *punishin'*."

Mrs. Roosevelt shook her head sadly. "Oh, dear, Senator. I really don't think—"

"Y' understand," the senator interrupted, "that I'm not sayin' my daughter is one-hundred-percent innocent. No. She has a wild streak in her."

"Resulting in?" asked Hopkins.

"Well . . . You all remember how Alice Roosevelt . . . Of course, you would remember, dear lady. Alice Roosevelt, the daughter of the late, great President Theodore Roosevelt, made a brilliant match. She married Nicholas Longworth, a most distinguished congressman from Ohio. He was in fact Speaker of the House durin' three terms. So— My daughter was engaged to marry Vernon Metcalf, another distinguished congressman from Ohio. And some way she . . . she let the engagement fail. I have my suspicions that Mr. Christopher Asman interfered with that."

"*Christian* Asman," Hopkins corrected him.

"A Christian he ain't," sniffed Senator Fisher.

"Just what Ohio district does Congressman Metcalf represent?" asked Mrs. Roosevelt.

"Suburbs of Cleveland, I b'lieve," said the senator.

Hopkins spoke. "Senator," he said. "I am sorry, but I don't believe I can fire Mr. Asman on the basis of what you have told us. I did secure his promise this morning that he will never contact your daughter again."

The promise did not mollify the senator. "See? Goes t'show," he said. "He never cared nothin' for her. He got all he wanted from her. So when he's told not to see her no more, does he protest his undyin' love? No. He jus' says, 'Wham-bam, thank ya, Ma'am,' an' walks away."

"Oh, Senator! I don't think it's quite that crude. Can't you suppose he just elected to obey a father's wishes?"

"If he was any kind of man at all, and cared for the girl, he'd say, 'Hell with daddy's wishes,' and go on seein' the girl. But it's not that way. He's a *seducer*! And he ruined her. Ruined her reputation, besides what else, and a woman doesn't have anything else as important as her reputation. So . . . I guess you've done all you're gonna do for me. I thank you for the hospitality."

Washington was no longer cold that Saturday afternoon, but it was wet. Warm wind coming up from the south, smelling of the sea and of an early spring accelerated the melting of last night's snow. Children who had seen the snow Friday evening and had expected to sled on it all day Saturday, moped after their mothers, who dragged them by the hands through stores as they did their shopping. Cars moving on the streets threw dirty water on cars parked along the curbs, until some of the parked cars were black with dripping grime.

In her office on the second floor, Mrs. Roosevelt stared at her pages of notes. The persistent Ohio connection was troubling. Everybody with any significant connection to the murder of Shondor Jack seemed to have come from Ohio.

A person could sit and stare at these notes for hours, without coming up with anything. Yet, she felt certain one or two of the facts she had written down had something to do with the solution to the mystery.

Why does Mr. Asman not wear his watch?

Who is JWP?

Christian Asman was the owner of what Mr. Szczygiel and Lieutenant Kennelly agreed in describing as a handsome and expensive gold pocket watch. Why did he not carry it?

It was inscribed JWP. Instinctively, the First Lady felt that was an important clue.

But what was proved by these two circumstances? She suspected she would come much closer to solving the mystery if she could explain the watch and its inscription.

Mr. Szczygiel and Lieutenant Kennelly were still on duty. When there had been a murder in the White House—resulting in an unsolved mystery—both of them would take no time off until the mystery was solved or—Well . . . They said they would give up after a time, but she doubted that.

Teddy O'Neil sat in her parlor, facing the two investigators with a look of amused contempt. She was dressed in a white nightgown and peignoir, and her lustrous red hair lay in brushed-out abundance over her shoulders. Her bright parlor was alive with blooming house plants, and two canaries chirped in their cages. She had kept the officers waiting almost half an hour, and Szczygiel had been interested in the reading material lying on her coffee table—the *American Mercury*, the *New Republic*, the *New Yorker*, and *Foreign Affairs*. He wondered if she read this kind of stuff or if she left it out for her clientèle to read.

"Shondor Jack? Damn right," she said.

"You knew him?"

"Knew him? I *know*—Wait a minute! Whatta you mean, *knew*? Don't tell me the guy . . ."

"He checked out," said Kennelly. "Wednesday night. Somebody put some extra holes in him."

"'Kay," she said, nodding. "So you guys figure I might have had something to do with it. Shee!"

"Why would we figure that, Teddy?" Kennelly asked.

She stared at him for a moment. "How'd you introduce yourself? Lieutenant Ed Kennelly, right? Well, Ed, let's don't play guessing games."

She had just put down a favorite police technique: using a person's first name, while remaining Officer This or Detective That. Either Teddy O'Neil had been questioned by the police many times, or she was just too smart to fall for that little trick.

"I'm not playing any games, Teddy, I assure you," said Kennelly.

"Then direct questions, directly answered," she said.

"Direct question," said Kennelly. "Did Shondor Jack pimp for you?"

"Direct answer," she said. "He wanted to, but he couldn't."

"Why couldn't he?"

She smiled and tossed her head. "I got protection," she said. "Do I have to say more?"

No, she didn't. Kennelly understood. She was saying she worked for another pimp, and if Shondor Jack tried to muscle in, he'd be taken out. If he hadn't been murdered in the White House, here was a dramatically important clue: somebody—Teddy's pimp—with a motive to kill Djaković, and that somebody would likely be the kind of guy who was capable of murder. But not in the White House.

"How did you come to know Shondor?" he asked.

"Cleveland," she said.

"You're from Cleveland?"

"Seems like another world, another century," said Teddy O'Neil. "But yeah. I'm from Cleveland. Rosa Zdravchev. Seven years ago Shondor Jack muscled me. He was fresh out of the Ohio Penitentiary and needed money. The quickest way he knew to get it was to threaten little girls. And here he was, in Washington, doing the same thing."

"You get in the business because of him?" Kennelly asked.

"Well . . . Yeah. Sort of. I wasn't . . . I was a sort of amateur before he muscled me."

"Can you account for Wednesday evening between, say, eight and ten?" Kennelly asked.

"Oh, sure," she sneered. "I was at a dinner for the Daughters of the Confederacy."

Ed Kennelly glanced at Stan Szczygiel and shrugged.

Szczygiel picked up the questioning. "Miss O'Neil," he said. "Christian Asman."

She stared at him for a moment. "Rumpelstiltskin," she said.

Szczygiel grinned. "Do you know Christian Asman?"

She picked up a package of Wings and struck a match to light one. "Sure," she said. "I know Chris. So?"

"Is he your pimp?"

She drew a long puff from her cigarette and blew a

stream of smoke through her nostrils. "Mr. Szczygiel," she said. "What would I want with a pimp?"

"You said you have protection."

"In my line of work, you have protection, or a guy like Shondor muscles in on you. I have insurance, you might say."

"Want to tell us the name of your insurance guy?" asked Kennelly.

"Deeter," she said. "You know him."

"And when Shondor Jack tried to muscle you?"

"Deeter persuaded him it wasn't a good idea."

"Did he stay persuaded?"

"Never saw him again."

"When did you see him last?"

She shrugged. "Say two months ago. But he wasn't muscling then. He just wanted a piece of information. You gotta understand that Shondor Jack was a realistic guy. He knew when he'd been shoved aside. He didn't resent it, really. He said to me, 'I see you got smart, kid.' He just wanted to know something."

"Wanted to know what?"

"Wanted to know if I'd seen a guy."

"What guy?"

"A guy named John Preston."

"Who's John Preston?"

"Damn 'f I know. A John. Back in the old days, when I was a kid, in Cleveland, Shondor claimed he'd set me up with this Preston character two or three times. Listen. Shondor kept my eyes black, my body bruised, that month or two I had to work for him. He kept me well supplied with hooch, and he gave me some reefers, too. I didn't know much about what was going on, that time. When they got him for Murder One, I was a happy little girl. He was locked up. I dropped the stuff he'd got me on—alcohol and reefers—and went to work independent. Then that lying little bitch got him off on the Murder One charge, and he comes chargin' out of jail loaded for bear. He broke my nose. Then . . . thank God—"

"Thank God?"

"They got him on something else. Burglary or something. And he went back in the crowbar hotel. That's when I left Cleveland. I figured he'd find some chippie to lie for him and get him off that one, too. I never saw the guy again until he showed up in Washington lately."

"How long had he been in Washington?" asked Kennelly.

"Don't know. I've been here five years. Nice town." She grinned mischievously at Kennelly. "You run a nice town. Just the right balance. A girl like me can make a living. A guy like Shondor Jack can't—can't, anyway, by thumping on the bodies of girls like me."

"Preston," said Szczygiel. "Who's Preston? And what did Shondor Jack want with him?"

Teddy O'Neil shook her head. "He didn't tell me. That wasn't Shondor's way, to take you into his confidence."

"When you knew this Preston in Cleveland, what was he? What kind of man was he?"

"I don't remember the guy. These days . . . These days I got a pretty good idea who my friends are. Not then. I don't remember this guy Preston at all, not to say who he was, what kind of guy he was, anything." She shrugged. "I just don't remember him. I wish there hadn't been so many of them that I can't remember one of them. But that's the way it is."

"Okay. Asman. Who's Asman?"

She shrugged. "A guy. He found out what I do for a living, and it intrigued him. He wants my body, but he doesn't want to pay for it."

"You have a relationship?"

"Yeah. One time. One time he paid. Now he buys me drinks. He likes to talk to me. He's a strange guy. He asked me one time if I ever thought of getting out of the business—and if I did, would I consider marrying him. Can you top that?"

Kennelly shook his head. "Damned if I know how to top that," he said.

Saturday evening. The President spent much of the day meeting with men from Capitol Hill, explaining the court-reform bill that had already been tagged, apparently irretrievably, with the epithet "court-packing." He had received gratifying assurances of support, but he knew by now that he faced an extremely difficult battle. A new coalition of forces was ranging against him: Worst of all, and in the lead, were "patriots" who were wrapping themselves in the flag and Constitution and setting out to preach a holy crusade.

"Who," he asked Missy LeHand and Grace Tully, who alone had joined him for his cocktail hour, "could honestly accuse me of want of respect for our constitutional traditions?"

The two young women shook their heads. He smiled at them and let them know by that smile that he didn't really expect an answer. They were loyal to him, so loyal they would not tell him even if they believed he was wrong.

The beautiful Grace Tully—whom he nicknamed "The Colleen"—was Missy's assistant. She *was* a lovely girl.

And her loyalty . . . Right now she had better things to do with her evening than sit and share a drink with her employer. Yet, here she was. Her loyalty included sacrificing her weekend.

And Missy—Lovely Missy . . . she had dedicated her life to him, and he hoped in some way to justify that dedication.

"'Nine old men,'" he muttered. "I wish I hadn't said it. That one little phrase puts a slant on everything."

"You said something better," said Grace.

"What do you like better, Colleen?"

"You said of the NRA decision, 'This takes us back to horse-and-buggy days.' People remember that."

Franklin Roosevelt grinned. He poured cocktails for his two secretaries.

"Where's Mrs. Roosevelt this evening?" Grace Tully asked.

"I believe," he said, "she is deeply involved in her Sherlock Holmes manifestation." He raised his glass to toast something: the two women, the idea of the First Lady playing detective, whatever— "Let us hope she makes another contribution to justice."

The First Lady was, in fact, with Stan Szczygiel and Ed Kennelly at a restaurant on Connecticut Avenue called Old New Orleans. It advertised by employing a plump black woman to sit in the window, dressed like a plantation mammy, and rock in a rocking chair, hour after hour. The cuisine, New Orleans though it might be called, was pure Washington—just about anything you wanted, so long as you wanted it fried in deep fat.

Although she was the best-known woman in America, it was still possible for Mrs. Roosevelt to go out in public and avoid being recognized. All she'd done this evening by way of an incognito was to wear a hat with a veil. It was surprising how so little a thing could block recognition. Although she received some curious stares in the restaurant, the two or three people who thought they recognized her were probably not sure. Anyway, the return stares of the two men discouraged sustained gawking.

One specialty of the restaurant was fried chicken. Another was quick service. Their food was soon before them: platters of fried chicken with mashed potatoes and yellow chicken gravy, and side dishes of buttered lima beans.

"I have begun to suspect we had better check into something," said the First Lady. "Mr. Asman's personnel file contains two letters of recommendation from lawyers in New York, who say they know him and endorse him as a capable attorney. One was written by a Mr. Jonathan Merrill, the other by a Mr. Melvin Shapiro. Rex Tugwell says he knows Mr. Merrill. Personally, I am going to ask Rex how well he knows him. But I suspect it might be wise if we looked a little more thoroughly into Mr. Asman's background."

"What do you expect to find out?" asked Szczygiel.

"I think we should not proceed in the *expectation* of finding anything. I think we should investigate and see what we can learn. But—I will acknowledge I should like to learn if there is any possibility of a Cleveland connection. Everyone else whose name figures in the case seems to have that connection."

"Well . . . Asman is from New York," said Kennelly.

"Yes," said Mrs. Roosevelt. "But I've wondered about something. When we asked Mr. Asman if he had ever been in Cleveland, he was most emphatic that he had never been there except in the railroad station. Do you recall? He was absolutely vehement about never having been in Cleveland, called it a stinking hole or some such words. Besides which, he slandered the Cleveland bar, saying no lawyer who amounted to much would ever consider practicing in that city. Do you remember?"

"I do, yes," said Szczygiel, and Kennelly nodded.

"Does it seem strange?" she asked. "Why should he have been so impassioned on the subject?"

"A good point," said Kennelly. "Maybe there is a Cleveland connection, and the last thing in the world he wants is for us to find out about it."

"A connection between Mr. Asman and Mr. Djaković," she mused. "A connection . . ."

"That would solve the case," said Szczygiel.

"Not necessarily," said Mrs. Roosevelt. "Now. I think we should focus also on the connection between Margaret Dempsey and Christian Asman. After all, both of them were in the vicinity of the Red Room Wednesday night. I not-quite promised not to tell you this, but there is a connection between Miss Dempsey and Shondor Jack."

The First Lady had, as she had just said, all but promised Margaret Dempsey that she would not tell the investigators about the young woman's appearance as an alibi witness for Shondor Jack. But she had not actually promised, of course, and what she had learned might be a key to the investigation.

"What is more," she said grimly, "in the same week that Djaković was acquitted, Margaret Dempsey deposited ten thousand dollars in an account in the Monongahela Bank. I am sorry that I cannot, in my own mind, satisfactorily resolve that coincidence."

"I'm sure the bank would not tell us where the money came from," said Kennelly.

"It's hardly likely to have been a check," said Szczygiel. "Cash, I would imagine. Then the bank wouldn't know where it came from."

"Who defended Shondor Jack at that trial?" asked Kennelly.

"Let's make a note to find out," said Mrs. Roosevelt.

They ate their chicken and mashed potatoes. The dinner was tasty, the First Lady noted, and for an instant she longed for the day when she could walk into any little restaurant anywhere, without a Secret Service escort, and eat a simple meal without becoming the subject of oppressive attention. For a few minutes, conversation parted from the Shondor Jack murder, and they talked about the snow and even about the Roosevelt children and what they were doing.

A uniformed police officer walked into the restaurant, looked around, spotted Kennelly, and approached their table. He was a sergeant. Kennelly rose and walked a step or two away from the table to talk to him. In a moment he returned.

"We can stop guessing about our suspect," he said bleakly. "Christian Asman is dead."

The police had cordoned off the alley, and it was possible for Kennelly to drive to within a few yards of where the body of Christian Asman lay on its back in a puddle of black water.

Neither Szczygiel nor Kennelly had been able to argue

the First Lady out of coming along. If, she said, the newspapermen were already there, she would simply sit in the car—and surely the D.C. police could keep the reporters away from a car. As it turned out, the press had not as yet been notified, police barricades kept people away, and no one stood staring at the body but half a dozen officers and the medical examiner. Mrs. Roosevelt was able to leave the car and—still half disguised by her veil and spectacles—approach the ghastly spectacle of the deceased man.

The medical examiner had no idea who the tall woman in the black coat and fox collar might be. He recognized Kennelly, though, and said briskly, "Well, there's no question at all about how this party got dead. Two bullets at close range, right in the chest."

"Robbery?" Kennelly asked one of the uniformed officers.

"Not unless somebody wasn't interested in the hundred bucks he was carrying," said the policeman.

Stan Szczygiel had taken Mrs. Roosevelt's arm, solicitously trying to keep her back as far as possible. She tugged him forward.

Asman had been killed in an alley. The puddle in which his body lay was just a hole in the pavement, broken by a garbage truck, probably. The back doors of bars and restaurants opened on both sides of the alley, and cans stood in cluttered ranks, waiting to be emptied into a truck.

"No overcoat, no raincoat," said Mrs. Roosevelt. "No hat. He must have stepped out the back door of one of these places."

In the second door away from the body, a man in the stained white clothes of a cook stood on a little concrete porch and smoked a cigarette. He watched the police at work around the inert body, but he showed little interest.

"Do people walk through the kitchens of places like these and out the back door?" asked the First Lady. "I suspect not."

"He could have walked in from the end of the alley," said Kennelly.

"Without hat and coat, on a night like this?" she asked. "I doubt it, Lieutenant Kennelly. No. I suggest an element of the investigation should be to find his hat and coat, which are almost certainly hanging in one of these restaurants or bars."

Kennelly grinned, but he would give the order.

Mrs. Roosevelt sighed. "I suppose this means we just start over from the beginning," she said.

"No," said Szczygiel. "We know a lot that we didn't Wednesday night."

"It is possible, I suppose," she said, "that the two murders are not connected."

"They are connected, Ma'am," said Kennelly. "I promise you that."

8

The next morning the President and Mrs. Roosevelt attended services at St. John's Episcopal Church. The sermon was satisfactorily bland and pleased the great majority of the parishioners. The First Lady said a silent prayer for the soul of Christian Asman. She tried to concentrate on the service and not to think of what circumstance had led to the death of the young lawyer.

At the suggestion of Harry Hopkins, he and not the President issued the White House statement on the death of a staff member: "'He was just the finest type of man you could imagine,' said Harry Hopkins, head of WPA and Asman's boss in the Executive Wing. 'I guess the chief regret the President and I have is that we didn't get to know him any better than we did. When a man does his work faithfully and competently, often you don't have much occasion to get personally acquainted with him.'"

The morning papers carried a brief account of Asman's death and printed the statement without comment. The *Post*, for example, said:

> Christian Asman, an attorney on the White House staff, was found dead last night in an alley between G and H streets. Police say Asman died of gunshot wounds. They have no suspect in the shooting.
>
> Asman, a graduate of Harvard and Harvard Law, was an attorney in New York City before joining the staff of the White House approximately a year ago. He was unmarried, and no family has been identified.
>
> Harry Hopkins, by whom Christian Asman was employed, said "He was just the finest type of man you could imagine . . ."

Back in her office on the second floor of the White House, Mrs. Roosevelt turned over a fresh page in her yellow tablet. Even before Stan Szczygiel and Ed Kennelly arrived, she had written a list:

Who might have killed Mr. Asman?
Senator Fisher (unfortunately).
Miss Fisher (very unlikely).
Congressman Metcalf (jealousy?).
Miss Dempsey (but why?).
What is connection with Miss O'Neil?
Who was "older woman" at Farragut?
Person not yet identified.

Kennelly nodded as he scanned the list. "We have our work cut out for us, hmm? So where do we start?"

"I suggest," said Mrs. Roosevelt, "that we simplify our work by eliminating the unlikely suspects first. It is highly unlikely, it is not, that Miss Fisher killed Mr. Asman. Even so, I suppose we are obliged to clear up any doubt on that score. We must know if Miss Fisher's relationship with Mr. Asman was the cause of the severance of the romantic relationship between her and Congressman Metcalf. If it was, then conceivably Congressman Metcalf resented that and— Well. You see what I mean."

Stan Szczygiel shook his head over the list. "It's that last entry that bothers me most," he said. "'Person not yet identified.' I've begun to think that half the population of Washington might have wanted to kill Christian Asman. After all—we have to face it—he wasn't really a very nice fellow."

"Do you want to read the autopsy report?" Kennelly asked.

"I don't like to read them," said Mrs. Roosevelt. "They are always so—"

"Clinical," said Kennelly.

She could not help but smile.

"Anyway, there are no surprises," said Kennelly. "Asman was killed by two shots from a thirty-eight caliber revolver, fired at close range. One bullet tore open the left side of his heart. The other went through his left lung. At the time of his death he had consumed enough alcohol to put his blood-alcohol level at oh-one-nine percent—which means he was drunk. Good and drunk."

"Did anyone find his coat and hat?" she asked.

"Yes. When everybody left the Hi-Ho Lounge, there was an extra hat and coat."

"'Hi-Ho Lounge.' Oh, dear!"

"Are there any witnesses to Mr. Asman's having been in the Hi-Ho Lounge? Did anyone see him leave?"

"We're checking. The bartender and the waitresses are scattered all over the city, it being Sunday. We'll talk to them tomorrow evening."

"Does it sound to you like a professional killing?" asked Mrs. Roosevelt.

"Well, whoever did it was calm and cool," said Kennelly.

"Sunday . . ." she said quietly. "I think you two gentlemen deserve the rest of the day off. I'm afraid there's not much we can do, anyway."

Maybe there wasn't much for them to do the rest of that day. But there was plenty for her.

That afternoon the First Lady attended an outdoor meeting on the Ellipse. It was held outdoors because the people who had come could not afford to rent a hall. They were farmers displaced by the combined tragedies of the Depression and the Dust Bowl. Not many could even afford to come to Washington. Many were there as representatives of friends and neighbors who had collected money to make it possible for them to come—and, even so, some of them had ridden in boxcars or hitchhiked. They had come in mid-winter because this was their slow season, when they could give their time to a visit to the capitol in hope of making the government hear their pleas.

They were there this winter to urge Congress to enact the Bankhead-Jones Farm Tenant Bill, which was designed, they had heard, to make it possible for them to make their living as farmers, the only thing they knew how to do, and get off the relief rolls.

There were only a few hundred of them. They were ragged. Some of them looked malnourished.

Mrs. Roosevelt talked with a girl who said she was eighteen years old. She was pregnant. Her bulging belly was not quite covered by a frayed black coat fastened with safety pins in place of missing buttons. She wore a pair of man's high-top shoes, several sizes too big for her. Her dirty hair was stringy, her complexion splotched.

"My dear, should you have come?" the First Lady asked. "In your condition, it might have been better if you had stayed at home."

"Home done come, Ma'am," said the girl.

"I . . . I'm sorry. How do you mean your home—?"

"We-uns live in our truck. Me and the ol' man and the baby . . . and th' other baby, comin'. Come from West Virginia. Ain' nothin' else to do. Ain' got no land no more. Ain' got no work. Might's well come see if we can argue for some help."

Secretary of Agriculture Henry Wallace was standing beside the First Lady, listening.

"Do you know who we are?" Mrs. Roosevelt asked the girl.

The girl shook her head.

"This is Mr. Wallace, Mr. Henry Wallace, the secretary of agriculture. And I am Mrs. Roosevelt."

The girl's mouth fell open, and she glanced back and forth between them; but the First Lady remained uncertain that the girl knew who she and Wallace were.

"We are going to do all we can to help you, dear. Everything we can. As quickly as we can."

Mrs. Roosevelt did not make a speech that day. In the damp cold of that February afternoon, she met and talked personally with nearly every one of the farmers and their wives.

On Monday morning the First Lady telephoned the Georgetown home of Senator John Fisher shortly after ten o'clock—when, she had surmised, the senator himself would have left the house for Capitol Hill. As she had anticipated, Joan Fisher answered. Mrs. Roosevelt asked her if she would mind stopping by the White House at her earliest convenience. Joan Fisher said she could be there in an hour. Her tone suggested that she suspected the invitation was actually a summons.

Mrs. Roosevelt spent that hour dictating her column and going through mail. The young woman was prompt and arrived by eleven.

Instinctively, the First Lady was prepared to like Joan Fisher. She was one of those striking blondes who might have been obtrusively spectacular; but she had subdued her appearance in a measured way that suggested she was embarrassed about being so beautiful, but couldn't help it. She had on a black knit wool dress, with skirt at mid-calf length as style dictated. She wore a strand of pearls and a small diamond in a gold setting on her right hand.

Conceding inwardly that her imagination might have escaped discipline, Mrs. Roosevelt thought she saw something more in Joan Fisher: that the young woman was a little cynical and world-weary, as well as discouraged and unhappy.

"I am sorry to have to ask you to come to see me on such an unfortunate occasion, Miss Fisher. I know the death of Mr. Christian Asman must distress you deeply."

Joan Fisher shrugged, as though the death of Asman

only added another element to a burdensome life. "He was a friend," she said quietly.

"Miss Fisher," said Mrs. Roosevelt a little more firmly, "I have to ask you some rather personal questions. I have asked you to come here, since I believe it will be easier for you to talk to me than it would be to talk to an investigator from the District Police."

"He was murdered," the young woman said dully.

"More than that, he was a suspect in another murder."

Joan Fisher's eyes widened. "Chris . . . My god, who could *he* have murdered?"

"For the moment, I will not answer that question. What I want to know is, can you think of anyone he might have wanted to kill?"

Joan Fisher shook her head slowly.

"Then, can you think of anyone who might have wanted to kill Mr. Asman?"

"My father, of course," she answered. "He threatened to do it."

"I feel I can hardly ask you if you think it's possible your father did it."

"Go ahead and ask me. I'll tell you. It's possible. I don't think he did, but he could have. Chris was killed—what? Eight-thirty or nine o'clock? My father was not at home. Saturday night is his poker night. They don't begin to play until nine. It's possible he shot Chris and went on to his poker game. Not likely, but possible."

"So you yourself were at home Saturday evening?"

"Do you think *I* killed him?"

"No. But we may as well hear you say you didn't."

"My father's poker night is my mother's bridge night," said Joan Fisher. "Three of her friends were at the house all evening. I serve their drinks and food."

Inwardly Mrs. Roosevelt was relieved: for the young woman, first, but also to have a name off her list of suspects.

"Your father says you were at one time engaged to marry Congressman Metcalf."

"Yes. We broke off the engagement about three months ago."

"I said I have to ask personal questions. Was your relationship with Mr. Asman the reason you and the congressman parted?"

"No, not really. I don't think you could say that."

"Were you seeing Mr. Asman when you were still engaged to Congressman Metcalf?"

Joan Fisher was becoming increasingly disturbed by the questions; whether from outrage over their violation of her privacy or because the questions were about to elicit something she didn't want to tell, Mrs. Roosevelt could not be certain. But the young woman's face had stiffened. Her lips were rigid.

"I began to see Chris when I was still engaged to Vern," she said curtly.

"Mr. Asman seems to have had a singular appeal to young women," said the First Lady. "I have become aware that he dated at least one other in the week before he died."

"Name your one other," Joan Fisher demanded.

"Correct me if I am mistaken," said Mrs. Roosevelt, "but I believe you were with Mr. Asman at the Farragut Bar on Thursday evening. He took you home in a taxi. Then—"

"We were being followed!"

"By the police," said the First Lady. "I told you Mr. Asman was suspected of murder. In any event, he took you home. Then he went to the Gayety Burlesque Theater, where he met a Miss Stormy Skye, a striptease dancer. He took her home, and she spent the night with him."

"Then I suppose," said Joan Fisher coldly, "that the police know I spent two hours in his apartment Friday evening."

"After he took you home that evening, he went to the Farragut Bar again, where he engaged for some time in a tête-à-tête with a young woman known to be a high-priced prostitute. He did not leave the bar with her, however."

Joan Fisher's lips trembled, and tears appeared in the corners of her eyes. "Chris was a— How shall I say it? Not a handsome man particularly. Nobody's knight in shining armor. But he was a *loving* man, a caring man, and he seemed so *lonely!* He was also a shy man. Yes, really. I wanted him to go to cocktail parties and so on. I remember trying to get him to go to a concert. I was going with Vern—Congressman Metcalf—and I offered to get a third ticket. Chris would not go. He was emphatic to the point of being offensive. He would not go."

"What was your relationship with him at this time?" Mrs. Roosevelt asked gently.

"I . . . I had already . . . had already been intimate with him once or twice. He had suggested it, most deferentially. And he had seemed . . . so much in need. So. My relationship was intimate."

"Am I old-fashioned, Miss Fisher, in wondering why you wanted your fiancé to meet socially with a man that—?"

"Not old-fashioned. No . . ."

"Were you in love with Mr. Asman?"

Joan Fisher drew a deep breath and for a very long moment hesitated before answering. "At one point," she whispered, "I suggested to Vern that we were not close enough to each other to be planning marriage. Then I suggested to Chris that I might break off my engagement and marry him. He— He wouldn't hear of it."

"Did Mr. Asman and Congressman Metcalf ever meet?"

Joan Fisher shook her head. "Never. At one point, Vern said he would like to meet this man who'd made such an impression on me; but Chris would not meet him, would not hear of it."

"Understandable, I suppose," said Mrs. Roosevelt.

Joan Fisher sobbed. "The last time I was with Chris—Friday evening, with the police watching outside—we talked about marriage. Vern had walked away in a huff, saying I was not sufficiently committed to him. I wanted to marry Chris. I—"

"You were, then, in love with him?"

Joan Fisher sucked in breath and stopped. "Well— I don't know. I . . . Oh, Mrs. Roosevelt, I don't know! We talked about it. He said he couldn't marry me. He said he couldn't, and he didn't say why. And I—"

"You weren't really sure you wanted to marry him."

The young woman nodded unhappily. "I don't know."

The First Lady had ordered refreshments, and this morning the pantry had been slow in sending it up. Now it arrived: a somewhat battered silver tray, from the Grant administration probably, with pots of coffee and tea, cream and sugar, cups and saucers. Joan Fisher accepted tea, with sugar and lemon.

"Miss Fisher," said the First Lady when both of them

had sipped tea, "have you ever heard the name Shondor Jack? Or the name Aleksandr Djaković?"

The young woman seemed to be revitalized by the tea—maybe by the business of holding the cup and saucer and stirring in sugar. She shook her head and said, "I have never heard either of those names, I am quite sure."

Mrs. Roosevelt thought for a moment. "A final question, I think. You have been most cooperative, and I appreciate it. Oh . . . Can you give me the names of your father's poker companions?"

"Only one of them," said Joan Fisher. "Most of them, over the years, have been totally unmemorable. But he plays from time to time with an officer I find interesting, who I believe was in Washington Saturday night. He plays with the group whenever he is in town."

"His name?"

"Lieutenant Colonel George Patton," said Joan Fisher.

Stan Szczygiel and Ed Kennelly appeared in Mrs. Roosevelt's office not long after Joan Fisher left.

"I am pleased to be able to say she has four alibi witnesses," said Mrs. Roosevelt. "Three besides her mother. I believe we can strike her from our list. Not her father. Not Congressman Metcalf. But Miss Fisher herself, I think we can."

Kennelly opened a fat briefcase. "We took the personal possessions from the Asman apartment," he said. "And there's something odd. When we searched quickly the other day we didn't find anything that named his family—not anybody, not any family at all. Now, searching more thoroughly . . . still nothing. It's like as if the guy was an orphan."

"His personnel record names a father and mother."

Kennelly shook his head. "With no addresses. The FBI office in New York City is looking for an 'F. C. Asman,' and so far hasn't come up with a thing. Not in the phone book. Hasn't been for ten years. No electric bill in that name. Nothin'. He said his family moved around a lot. Well, it looks like they've moved out of New York City."

"I am sorry I wasn't more forthcoming in telling you what I have begun to suspect," said Mrs. Roosevelt. "I strongly doubt that Mr. Christian Asman was really Mr. Christian Asman. I think he was somebody else—from Cleveland."

"Why," asked Szczygiel, "would two respectable New York lawyers—Jonathan Merrill and Melvin Shapiro—write letters of recommendation saying he was?"

"I should be interested to know," she said. "It is all but inconceivable that all these people have a Cleveland connection—and, more than that, a connection with Aleksandr Djaković."

"We are no closer than we were Wednesday night last week in finding out who killed Shondor Jack," said Szczygiel.

"Let me resolve one little problem very quickly," said the First Lady. She picked up the telephone and asked the White House operator to place a call to Professor Felix Frankfurter at the Harvard School of Law. "This should be easy," she said.

"I know what you have in mind," said Szczygiel. "I'm not sure knowing the answer is going to make things any simpler."

While she waited for the call to go through, the First Lady picked up her pad and amended an entry:

Who might have killed Mr. Asman?

Senator Fisher (unfortunately).

~~Miss Fisher (very unlikely).~~

Congressman Metcalf (jealousy?).

The operator reported she had found Professor Frankfurter, had called him out of a class to take a call from the White House. He was waiting on the line.

"Oh, Felix, I am so sorry to have interrupted—"

"Not at all, Eleanor. What can I do for you?"

"I need a bit of information from the college records," she said. "A Mr. Christian Asman. A-S-M-A-N. I need to know if he graduated from Harvard Law."

"When?"

"Oh, as long as ten years ago. Maybe more lately, but not within the past five years."

"Easily discovered," said Frankfurter. "I have here the printed alumni directory through—Asman, you say? A-S-M-A-N?"

"Mr. Christian Asman."

"Uh . . . No. No one by that name ever graduated from Harvard law. Not, anyway, through nineteen thirty-five."

Mrs. Roosevelt glanced at Szczygiel and Kennelly. "I see. Well, I thank you, Professor. I am most grateful."

"Anything I can ever do for you, Eleanor, I am at your service," said Professor Frankfurter.

The First Lady turned to Szczygiel and Kennelly. "I believe we have just learned something extremely important," she said.

* * *

The War Department was able to assure the First Lady that Lieutenant Colonel George Patton had not yet left Washington.

When she told the War Department duty officer that Lieutenant Colonel Patton was invited to share cocktails with the President and Mrs. Roosevelt at the White House at six, the officer assured her he could locate Colonel Patton and advise him of this.

The President was surprised.

"Who? Never heard of him. Some . . . professional soldier? You have to understand something, Babs. When an army officer is invited to break bread—tip a sip or three of gin—with the President of the United States, this President or any other, it fouls up the army pecking order—and, to the United States Army, even defense of the country takes second place to pecking order. The only place in the world, with the possible exception of the United States Navy, where pecking order is more important is Vatican City! And you've invited a lieutenant—"

"The man may have a minor clue to the solution of two murders," she said.

"Well, tomorrow he'll be the most talked-about lieutenant colonel in the army. But you've invited him, so I suppose there's no stopping him. But remember, Babs, in future: In our nation's military and naval establishment, hierarchy is all."

The President nevertheless welcomed Lieutenant Colonel George Patton as if it had been his own idea to invite him for cocktails at the White House. The single unusual aspect of the occasion was that the President had invited no one else except Missy and Harry Hopkins. It was unusual, too, for Mrs. Roosevelt to be present during the President's evening cocktail hour, which she usually avoided.

Patton surprised everyone by appearing in uniform. He had attained the temporary rank of lieutenant colonel in 1918 and had only recently reached it again as permanent rank, but appearing in uniform allowed him to wear his decorations: the Distinguished Service Cross, the Distinguished Service Medal, and a Purple Heart.

After the President expressed himself about the seemliness of inviting Patton to the White House, Mrs. Roosevelt had made two calls to find out who he was—apart from an officer who played poker with Senator Fisher on Saturday nights.

He was, she had discovered, a man who had chosen to become a soldier, despite having a background that included ample family money. He might have decided to go into business. His army superior had told her George Patton was "a man of limited capacities, frankly said, but a man whose limited capacities are for soldiering. He soldiers well. I'm not sure he could do anything else, no matter how hard he tried."

The President had not been told that, and so met Patton with no preconceived ideas as to who or what he was.

He was favorably impressed, though, when the lieutenant colonel expressed himself as a long-time devotee of martini cocktails and suggested the President try mixing them at a ratio of nine to one. "It makes them a bit strong, Sir," he said, "but when we remember that the ice melts and dilutes them, a stronger ratio is justified.

This assumes, of course, that one does not gulp them down but sips them, allowing the ice to melt."

"To melt?" the President asked, frowning curiously.

"Yes, Mr. President," said the lieutenant colonel. "Let us not forget that a proper martini has *three* ingredients, not just two."

"Three?"

"Yes, Sir. Gin, vermouth, and water. The water is from the melting ice. I have a friend, Mr. President, who thought he could make the best possible martini by pouring a bit of vermouth into a bottle of gin and chilling that gin in the refrigerator. Sir, the martinis he poured out of that bottle were undrinkable. The water from the melting ice is the ingredient that takes the harsh edge off a martini. Omit that water, Sir, and it is not a gentleman's drink but a hairy beast."

The President laughed heartily. "I knew I shook them for some reason! I guess I didn't know why! I am grateful to you, colonel. I will try your nine-to-one ratio and shake until much of that ice is melted. And that, I imagine you guarantee, will give us the perfect martini."

"Mr. President," said Patton, "solving the puzzle of the perfect martini is like trying to square the circle. We strive and strive, we improve and improve, but I doubt we have achieved, or will achieve, the perfect martini."

"Colonel Patton," said the President, laughing, "I am grateful to my wife for having brought to my cocktail hour a true connoisseur of that glorious drink, the martini."

"A cavalry officer, Sir," said Patton, "has to find something to think about to take his mind off horses."

"Yes. Definitely. You served with Pershing, I understand."

"In Mexico, Sir, and then in France."

"Pershing," said the President. "A most distinguished general. He is, I imagine, the best you ever met."

"Actually not, Mr. President," said Patton after he had taken a tiny sip from his drink.

"Oh? Who greater, Colonel?"

"Napoleon, Sir."

"Oh, yes. Well . . . But my comment was about military leaders you have met, maybe served under."

"I served under the Emperor, Sir," said Colonel Patton blandly, in the tone of a man absolutely sure of himself. "I was one of his marshals."

President Roosevelt's eyes flicked to his wife's, then to Missy's and to Hopkins's. "Well, uh, sure. You are so familiar with Napoleon's campaigns, through your education, that you—"

"Begging your pardon, Mr. President," said Patton. "I discuss what I am about to discuss only with people who . . . only with people whom I can trust *and* people with imagination. You see, I believe in reincarnation. I believe I have been a soldier since mankind emerged and appointed some men soldiers. I was with the Pharaohs. I fought under Alexander, under Julius Caesar, under Charlemagne . . . My recollection of battles is too vivid, too detailed to have been gained from history books." He smiled and shrugged: a disarming gesture that did not apologize and asked no one to apologize for not believing him. "I am certain of all this," he went on. "I am as certain it is true as you are certain it is not."

"Fair enough," said Harry Hopkins. "It makes as much sense as what some people believe and call religion."

Colonel Patton smiled again and again nodded. Mrs.

Roosevelt had noticed that his uniform was exquisitely tailored. The colonel, she understood, had substantial outside income, and he and his wife lived well wherever duty sent him.

"I need to ask you a question, Colonel Patton," she said.

"Of course, my dear lady," he said.

"I believe that when you are in Washington you play poker on Saturday nights with a group that meets at the Army-Navy Club."

"I do, Ma'am," he said. "Not always, because sometimes I bring my wife with me, and on those weekends we enjoy other sorts of engagements."

"Last Saturday night?" she asked.

"Poker at the Army-Navy Club," he said.

"Yes. Now, then . . . Did Senator Fisher play poker with you Saturday evening?"

"He did."

"At what time did he arrive for the game, Colonel?"

"Oh, say nine o'clock. Yes. I'd say nine o'clock. Is there any particular significance to that?"

"Can you tell me anything about his condition when he arrived?" she asked. "Was he—?"

"Drunk? No, Ma'am. The Senator may have been a little wobbly when he left, three or four hours later, but he was sober as a judge when he came in."

9

Agent Stan Szczygiel was on the telephone to New York. He had left word with the receptionist that the White House was calling Mr. Jonathan Merrill, who was "in conference."

"Tell him to call the White House when he is out of conference," Szczygiel had left it.

And now Jonathan Merrill was calling—Jonathan Merrill, who had written a letter of recommendation for his Harvard classmate Christian Asman. A letter, that is, for a man Harvard had no record of.

"H'lo. Jonathan Merrill heah. Is this the White House? Who's calling, please?"

"Not the President, Mr. Merrill."

"Oh, no. No! No . . . I s'pose not."

"My name is Stanlislaw Szczygiel. I am an agent of the Secret Service.

"Szczygiel. Secret Service. Yaas. What can I do for you?"

"I'm calling about Christian Asman."

"Asman? I don't believe I know the name."

"I have in my hand a letter of recommendation, supposedly written by you, supposedly signed by you."

"Ah . . . Ah, yes! Asman. Of course. Yes, of course. Classmate of mine. Indeed, I wrote him a letter of recommendation. Certainly. Yes."

"Are you aware that he is dead?"

"Dead? Asman? No! Poor chap. Heart?"

"He was murdered, Mr. Merrill."

"Murdered! Oh, no! How could that be?"

"That's what we're trying to find out. At the moment we're having difficulty even locating a family for him. I thought maybe you could help with that."

"Uhmm . . . Well, actually I don't believe I ever met any of his family. No. I'm sure I didn't."

"Was he associated with a law firm there in New York?"

"No, I . . . I don't believe he was. Practiced law alone, I think."

"Your letter reads, 'Christian Asman was a classmate of mine at Harvard and has practiced law with distinction in New York City.' But you seem not to have known him very well, Mr. Merrill."

"Not terribly well, I suppose. No, not terribly well. You understand that one writes these letters as a matter of course. I do them from time to time. Matter of course. I didn't know the chap terribly well. Whoever would receive my letter would understand that. If the man graduated from Harvard Law, he merited a recommendation, by definition—and that's the basis on which I gave it."

"I see. Well, then, thank you Mr. Merrill."

Szczygiel put down the telephone. He wrote a note for Mrs. Roosevelt:

> Jonathan Merrill remembers Asman as a Harvard classmate—curious, in view of the fact that Harvard has no record of a student named Christian Asman. I haven't been able to reach Melvin Shapiro, but will try again in the morning.

Detective Lieutenant Ed Kennelly's interest had returned to something that had intrigued him before but had little significance until Asman was murdered. He laid out on his desk the envelope in which he had carried the wads of long dark hair he had found in the drains of Asman's bathroom.

Not Joan Fisher's hair, for sure. Not Stormy Skye's. Not Teddy O'Neil's. Another woman's, someone who had washed her hair in Asman's bathroom basin; also, apparently, in his bathtub.

It could be Margaret Dempsey's. Her hair was dark brown. Where had *she* been Saturday night? He would find out.

On the other hand, it seemed very likely there was still another woman. Millie, the waitress at the Farragut Bar, had spoken of "an older woman." Mrs. Roosevelt had considered that important enough to include the "older woman" on her list of suspects. It was important enough for Kennelly to return to the Farragut yet again.

He arrived there about nine, this time without Stan Szczygiel. The place was bustling. If anyone gave a thought to the man who had frequented the place, had sat at the same table night after night, no one showed it. Kennelly spoke to Millie:

"You know he's dead?"

She nodded. "I saw that in the newspaper. Scary. One night he's here, sitting over there . . . next night, he's dead."

"Was he here Saturday night?"

"No. After all, how could he?"

"Well, he could have come in earlier, met someone, gone out."

She glanced around; then shook her head emphatically. "You got me lookin' for the guy—you and your questions. No. He was not in here Saturday night."

"Okay. When we talked before, you told me he sometimes sat over there with somebody you called 'an older woman.' I need to know who that was."

"Dunno," she said. "I got no idea."

"How old?"

"Well . . . not so awful old, I guess. Looked old. Yeah. Looked older than that blonde he sat with. Looked older than Teddy O'Neil."

"How often did he see her?"

"More often than the others."

"Did she leave here with him?"

"For sure."

Kennelly glanced around the bar. "Not here tonight, I suppose?"

Millie shook her head. "I don't know . . . I guess I could say she never came in here except when she was meetin' him."

"What else can you tell me about her? Anything?"

"One thing—She got awful drunk. Sometimes when they left here, he was just about carryin' her."

Kennelly picked up Stan Szczygiel, who had emphatically asked to be included in this part of the investigation, and drove him to the Hi-Ho Lounge.

This place was a dive. Lover that he was of cheap, stinking cigars, Stan Szczygiel almost retreated from the heavy, smoky atmosphere of the Hi-Ho. The stench of burning tobacco was weighted with the smells of beer and whiskey, plus the unsubtle odors of unwashed clothes and bodies.

Kennelly was direct. He walked to the bar, showed his badge to the bartender, and asked, "Who's the boss?"

A short, heavyset, bald man in a white shirt, black bow tie, and black trousers came along the bar in response to this question and introduced himself as Alphonse Tranquillo, proprietor of the lounge.

"Make ya a fast, direct deal," said Kennelly brusquely. "I can stand right here and see enough violations to close you a month. If I look around, I can do better. You wanta stay open, Alphonse?"

Tranquillo shrugged. "I got friends," he muttered.

"Who won't do you a grain of good when the chips are down," said Kennelly.

"You want sumpin'," said Tranquillo. "Name it."

"The guy that got killed out back Saturday night," said Kennelly. "I wanta talk about him."

Stan Szczygiel was no innocent, but this bar was beyond his experience. The only word that came to his mind was "tough." It was a joint, a tough joint. He wondered why Christian Asman would have come here.

Alphonse Tranquillo was responding to Kennelly's question with an elaborate, protracted shrug.

"He's not your usual customer," said Kennelly.

"Clerks and mechanics," said Tranquillo, dividing the population of Washington into the two categories used by the desk clerks at police headquarters. To them, everyone in Washington was either a clerk or a mechanic—

meaning a bureaucrat or a manual laborer—nothing else. "Me, I get the mechanics."

"Which," said Kennelly, "is why you would have noticed a clerk like Asman. A lawyer. A government lawyer, dressed like a government lawyer. He came in here, hung up his hat and coat, and went out the back door into the alley, leaving the hat and coat. Usual, Alphonse? You get a lot of government lawyers like that?"

"I get all kinds of people running in and out," said Tranquillo. "What ya think? You figure I can keep track of all of 'em, even if I wanted to, which I don't?"

"I figure you keep a pretty good eye open," said Kennelly. "A man in your line of business has to. What you got here, Alphonse? Prostitution? Gambling? And what would I find out if I took an inventory of the booze on the premises and compared it to what you've legally bought? Don't crap around with me, Alphonse. Not only can I close you two minutes from now, permanently, I can put your butt behind bars."

If Alphonse Tranquillo was frightened, he was capable of hiding it. "What can I do for ya, boss?" he asked.

"Who did Asman meet here?"

"I tell you true. I don't know. You're right I keep an eye on strangers that come in. Yeah, I sort of noticed your guy—if we're talkin' about the same guy. Yeah, I sort of noticed he talked with some broad a minute or two. An' I tell you true, Lieutenant, if that broad was standin' at the bar right now, two stools from us, I wouldn't know her. I honest to God wouldn't know her, boss. An' since I don't know her, would I be protectin' her? Not hardly likely."

"But he did meet a broad," said Kennelly.

"I can't say he met her. I say I noticed him talkin' to a broad."

"Describe her."

"Nothin' special, I swear. Ordinary-lookin' broad. Y' know, they come in here; you can't tell one from another specially, unless she's something special. Nothin' special."

"You'd know her if you saw her again, of course."

"Can't promise that," said Tranquillo. "I honestly didn't pay her no mind. Like I said, that was because she wasn't nothin' special."

"Do your customers ordinarily go out the back door?"

"Not very much. But the pee-pees are back there, on each side of the hall. Somebody goes back that way, it don't attract no attention."

"I'd like for you to come down to the morgue and have a look at the body," said Kennelly.

"Oh God, Mister, don't ask me to do that. Show me a picture or somethin'. I can't hardly stand to look at stiffs. They scare me."

Making him look at the body of Christian Asman produced nothing but what looked like a genuine shudder from Alphonse Tranquillo, plus what appeared to be a bona fide threat to vomit.

The body was pallid, like any two-day-old corpse; and without eyeglasses and the dignity of clothes, it was not immediately recognizable as that of Christian Asman. Kennelly knew that and had compelled Tranquillo to view it only in the hope the sight would make him reveal something new.

It didn't.

Though the wounds had been washed clean, they

were still conspicuous—as were the gaping incisions where the body had been cut open for the autopsy and then shoved back together. It was, in fact, a ghastly sight, and Tranquillo was not the only one sickened by it; Szczygiel paled and stepped back.

"There's the answer to his fatal fascination for women," said Kennelly cynically, nodding toward the groin. "Anyway, Alphonse, is he the guy who was in your bar Saturday night?"

"God knows," said Tranquillo, crossing himself.

"Well, is he or isn't he?"

Tranquillo choked. "Boss," he said, "I couldn't tell ya if I ever saw this guy before. If he was my brother, I wouldn't know him. Lemme out of here, God's sake, before I throw up."

Kennelly glanced around the cold, brightly lit room. He swept his arm around, gesturing toward the lockers where corpses lay out of sight, ready to be pulled out on sliding trays and displayed to witnesses—as Asman now was.

"We've got quite a collection here," he said. "Most nights. It's what makes this job so great."

"Boss," said Tranquillo, "I wouldn't have your job for any money in the world."

"Which means you'll help the guy that has to do it, when you can," said Kennelly. "Right?"

Tranquillo turned away from the body. "Right," he whispered hoarsely. "Sure. Sure, Lieutenant. I swear I've told you all I know. Can I help it if some guy winds up getting killed in the alley behind my joint? I got nothin' to do with it."

"Okay," said Kennelly. "I got another one I want you to look at.

"Hey! Hey, man, really!"

Kennelly shoved the corpse of Christian Asman back into its locker. He pulled out another drawer and flipped the covering off the body of Aleksandr Djaković—Shondor Jack.

"Him I know," said Tranquillo. He turned his back on the corpse. "Don't have to stare at him. I know who he is."

Kennelly covered the body and pushed it back in its locker. He led the way to the door and out of the refrigerated room. "So who is the guy?" he asked.

"Don't know his name. But he was a hustler, a small-timer. He was a pimp, for one thing. I figure he was in some other line, too; and sometimes he'd score and be loaded with money, which most times he didn't have much of. He was around the joint once or twice a week. Drank a lot. He wanted to run a tab, and when I said no to that he said he'd punch my lights out. I threw his ass out in the alley. That was two, three months ago. He never came back."

"When did he first start coming in your place?"

"Couldn't say exactly. Couple of years ago, I figure."

"Who'd he talk to mostly, when he came in?"

Tranquillo sighed loudly. "Well . . . Mostly with a guy that books bets. Horses. I heard 'em arguing about that, too. The guy back in there, the stiff, wanted more credit from the guy that takes the bets."

"What's the bookie's name?"

"MacMillan," said Tranquillo. "Called Mac."

"Is he in your joint tonight?"

"Figure he is."

"Let's go see him," said Kennelly.

* * *

Mrs. Roosevelt had chosen the Green Room for her meeting with Representative Vernon Metcalf. They sat in wing chairs to either side of the fireplace, where a small, cheerful fire crackled. A pot of coffee, with accoutrements, sat on a silver tray on the small, low table between them.

"I thought it more discreet to invite you here in the evening," she said to the congressman. "Also, I thought it might be less unpleasant if a rather disagreeable subject were raised by me rather than the somewhat gruff men who are investigating the murder of Mr. Christian Asman."

"I appreciate both thoughts," said Congressman Metcalf.

He was a tall, handsome young man with expressive, bulging blue eyes. A wisp of his light-brown hair had fallen down across his forehead, and he had not troubled himself to push it back.

"I know," said Mrs. Roosevelt, "that you were engaged to be married to Miss Fisher, and that you broke off the engagement, possibly because of her relationship with Mr. Asman."

The congressman nodded gravely. "That is true."

"What do you think was the relationship between Miss Fisher and Mr. Asman?"

Representative Metcalf drew a deep breath and held it for a moment. His face reddened. "At first," he said, "it was a simple friendship. I could not object to her having a male friend, although I did think it odd that I never met him."

"Yes, she made a point of that. Mr. Asman, it seems,

did not want to see you. He would have been embarrassed, I suppose."

"At first he would have had nothing to be embarrassed about. Then . . . Well, the nature of the relationship changed. I think I need hardly describe how."

"This is not just a suspicion on your part?" asked the First Lady. "I mean, jealousy sometimes leads to—"

"I followed them one night," said the congressman bluntly.

"So you broke off the engagement."

"She likes to think that she broke it off, at least that it was by mutual agreement. She explained that she had found someone who cared more for her than I did. She wanted to marry Asman. Then she found out he wouldn't marry her. Even so, she was devoted to him. Obviously I could not continue to be engaged to her, much less to marry her."

"I am compelled to ask you two questions," said Mrs. Roosevelt solemnly. "In the first place, weren't you quite upset with Mr. Asman? That is to say, weren't you jealous of him, didn't you resent him?"

Congressman Metcalf put his coffee cup on the tray. "I would be less than candid if I denied that," he said.

"Then of course the next question is, can you account for your evening, that is for Saturday evening?"

"I had dinner with one of my congressional aides, a young man who is leaving me, so it was a sort of farewell dinner. I left him about eight o'clock and went home. I spent the rest of the evening reading and listening to the radio."

"There is, then, no witness to your whereabouts after about eight o'clock?"

He shook his head. "No." Then he smiled. "I could

have gone to that alley and shot Asman. That's right. I could have. Some of the elements would have been a little difficult. For example, how was I to know where he was? And, frankly, I'd seen him only at a distance the night I followed him and Joan, so I didn't really know what he looked like. But, so far as my being able to prove I was somewhere else when he was shot . . . I can't."

"Oh, dear," said Mrs. Roosevelt. "I wish you could."

Mac MacMillan, the bookmaker was very much the kind of man Ed Kennelly had expected to see: a fellow with a sort of sporting look, wearing a loud, checkered sport jacket, an open-necked white shirt, and black-and-white shoes even though it was February. His yellow-gray hair was swept back over his head in oily waves. He wore octagonal glasses and held a toothpick in the corner of his mouth.

"Shondor Jack?" he said. "Yeah. Figured somethin' had happened to him. Don't see a guy for a week, you figure somethin' happened to him."

"Did he owe you money?" asked Kennelly.

"Two bills," said MacMillian."

"So you were looking for him."

"You better believe it."

Tranquillo had offered drinks on the house to Stan and Ed. He had even gone so far as to retrieve what he called "the good stuff" from a back room and had poured Stan a double shot of Beefeater's gin on the rocks. Ed was sipping on a Tennessee sour mash whiskey.

While Kennelly talked with the bookie, Szczygiel observed, sharp-eyed, what was going on around them.

People were trading in everything society professed to condemn. He watched curiously, but also with a surprising and profound sense of regret: regret because he had lost interest in most of what they were trading. It said something of a man that he could stand at a bar sipping gin and watch a commerce like this and not resolve to return and take part in it when he was off duty. He wondered if Ed did. Half-filled with reminiscent sadness, Szczygiel turned and concentrated on the conversation between Kennelly and MacMillan.

"You had reason to want the son of a bitch dead," said Kennelly.

MacMillan shook his head. "For two bills? Not worth the risk."

"Yeah, but a guy like you can't let two bills get away from him—then let the word get around that a guy got away with owing you."

"So where was Shondor killed and when? Maybe I better get my witnesses together."

"Gonna change the subject," said Kennelly. He withdrew from his pocket a photograph of Christian Asman. "Recognize?"

MacMillan shook his head. "I never saw that guy before in my life," he said.

"Okay. Back to Shondor. He was in trouble, hmm? With you. Maybe with other guys. Right?"

"Don't know about other guys. He owed me. I been known to have a guy busted up for two bills . . . but dead— No. It'd be dumb."

"You didn't have him busted up either," said Kennelly.

"Naw," said MacMillan with a smile. "Naw, I was a sucker. The guy kept promisin' me he was about to make the big score. This month, he said. This month he'd make the big score. He'd pay my two bills and give me ten times the action he'd give before."

"How many guys give you that kinda talk?"

"Every guy gives me that kinda talk," said MacMillan. "But this guy . . . I dunno. I guess I sort of believed him. Hey, he was an old-fashioned hustler. The guy had been around. Been around. Y'know? His kind, they usually good for what they owe, sooner or later. I just figured him for good, sooner or later."

"Give you any idea about what the score was gonna be?"

MacMillan turned down the corners of his mouth and shook his head. "Somethin' different," he said. "Like maybe a once-in-a-lifetime proposition."

Ed Kennelly stiffened. "Specific, Mister," he said. "Don't mess around with me. *Exactly*!"

Mac MacMillan smiled lazily. "Mess around with you? I'd have to be outa my mind to mess around with you, Kennelly. You know who I am. I know who you are. Mess around? Dumb, man. I'd have to be dumb. And dumb is one thing I ain't."

"So, talk!"

"Hey, would a two-bit lifetime professional chiseler like that tell me what he had in mind? All I can tell you is, he said he was lookin' for a big score. It was gonna be soon." The bookmaker shrugged. "But he was into me for two bills, and I figured that was plenty. I wouldn't put any more on the cuff."

"'Looking for a big score,'" said Mrs. Roosevelt. "And died before he made it." She shook her head. "In the death of Shondor Jack we had too few suspects—just Mr. Asman. In Mr. Asman's death we have too many. We may, I assume, eliminate people like this Mr. MacMillan as a suspect. After all, how could he have entered the White House?"

Stan Szczygiel shook his head. "How could Shondor Jack have entered the White House? If he could get in, so could Mac MacMillan."

"So could damn near anybody," said Kennelly.

It was nearly midnight. Szczygiel had telephoned the First Lady, as she had insisted he must, to report what he and Kennelly had done during the evening. She had suggested they come by, and she would have something good sent up from the pantry. They sat at a big table down in the White House kitchen over platters of scrambled eggs, bacon, toast, marmalade, and steaming coffee. It was just what the two men–and the First Lady herself, for that matter—needed. She herself conceded she was hungry. For a moment she had been tempted to wake the President and offer him the same midnight meal, but she had decided he needed his sleep more than he needed food at this hour.

It was Joyce Carter's duty night in the kitchen: the young woman who had said that Asman had invited her to go to bed with him. She sat at another table, apart from the First Lady and the two men, and watched them for any sign they wanted something more to eat. To her immense surprise, Mrs. Roosevelt had broken the eggs and sloshed them around in the big skillet with a fork while she, Joyce, was making coffee. She could not believe that the First Lady had taken part in the cooking. She wondered now if Mrs. Roosevelt would even assist in washing the dishes.

"Senator Fisher's time is not accounted for when Mr. Asman was murdered," said the First Lady over her eggs and coffee. "He actually threatened to harm Mr. Asman—though I am not at all sure we should take that seriously. Representative Metcalf admits that he resented Mr. Asman's intrusion on his engagement. He admits, also, that his time cannot be accounted for when the murder took place. Gentlemen, I . . . I find it difficult to think that either of them could have murdered—"

"Mrs. Roosevelt," Kennelly interrupted firmly. "Are you certain—I mean absolutely certain—that your class prejudice does not—"

"My *class prejudice*, Lieutenant?"

"Forgive me, but you don't like to believe that someone of your own social class could have—"

"I believe I am not so prejudiced, Lieutenant," she said coldly.

"I believe you are, Mrs. Roosevelt, if you will forgive me," said Kennelly. "You don't like to believe that Joan Fisher or Margaret Dempsey or the senator or the congressman could be the murderer. You didn't even like to think of Asman as a suspect. You would like to believe Shondor Jack was killed by one of his own class and maybe that one of that class then killed Asman."

"I am *not* prejudiced, Lieutenant," she said.

"No. Neither am I." He glanced at Joyce Carter. "I'm not either, but when a crime is committed, particularly in certain neighborhoods, I look for a Negro, not for a white man. I don't like to think that my own kind commit crimes, especially not crimes of violence."

Szczygiel spoke. "I think I should defend—"

"You don't have to defend," said Kenelly sharply. "I am not accusing Mrs. Roosevelt of looking away from evidence. I'm only saying—" He was now speaking to her, "—that you would be more comfortable if you could hang this crime on types like MacMillan. Well, it won't work. *I* think Shondor Jack was killed by Asman. And then someone, for some reason, killed Asman."

For a long moment Kennelly stared at his plate, while Szczygiel stared at him.

Mrs. Roosevelt nodded. "I cannot," she said, "dispute you on anything you have said. In fact, I am beginning to suspect something more. *I* am not defending Mr. Asman, Lieutenant Kennelly. Indeed, I think Mr. Asman killed Shondor Jack. And so far as social class is concerned, I am beginning to think a class conspiracy may well be an element of this case. I have begun to think that members of what you consider my social class are conspiring to conceal the truth in this case."

"Mrs. Roosevelt . . ." said Kennelly, his voice breaking with apology.

"No, Lieutenant," she said. "I have begun to develop a theory of this case that goes very much along the class line you have suggested. I disagree with you only wherein you say *I* share that prejudice." She paused, frowned. "And maybe you are right that I do. I am not angry with you for bringing it to my attention. I shall make a point of examining my attitudes."

"Your theory, Ma'am?" said Szczygiel. "May we know your theory?"

She shook her head. "No. I have begun to form an idea of how this whole tragic case developed. But it is theory, supposition. I would much rather have you two gentlemen pursuing your own ideas, independently. Among us we may come to one that solves the problem. Meanwhile, I would rather none of us convey our theories to the others."

"I apologize . . ." murmured Kennelly.

"Please don't, Lieutenant. Ed . . . If you defer to me, I shall prove to be an impediment to our solving this case. If you become reluctant to speak frankly to me, I shall have to withdraw and leave you to work on your own. I want to *help*, not to dominate your investigation."

"I'd hate to lose your ideas," said Kennelly. "They've always been damned good."

"At best they add an unorthodox point of view to your professionalism," she said. "That can be helpful sometimes. I hope it is now."

When the two men left, Mrs. Roosevelt remained in the kitchen. She did not offer to wash the few dishes they had used, but she sat and talked with Joyce Carter while Joyce washed them.

"You know that Mr. Asman is dead," said the First Lady.

"I know," said Joyce Carter quietly.

"Did you know we very much suspect he killed the man in the Red Room last Wednesday evening?"

Joyce Carter nodded.

"When he sat here and ate that evening, did you notice anything different about him?"

The girl thought for a moment. "No . . . No, not really."

"You are hesitant. Maybe you are thinking of something not important enough to tell me. But tell me anyway. Any little thing."

"Well . . . He was a little different, one way. He would come in . . . There was two kinds of ways. Sometimes—most times, really—he asked for sandwiches, and he took them back to his office. Other times he sat down here and ate. When he sat here, that's when he'd josh. You know, he'd make jokes."

"Was it only a joke when he asked you to go home with him?" asked Mrs. Roosevelt.

"No, Ma'am, he was serious about that. He only mentioned it when we were alone. No big grin with that. He meant it all right."

"But you never—"

"No, I never."

"I'm sorry. You were going to tell me what was different about him."

"Maybe it was nothin'. But what he did that was different, he kept lookin' at his watch, like he had to be someplace at a particular time. He'd fish out his watch and—"

"A pocket watch?"

"Yes. He didn't wear a wrist watch. He'd fish his watch out of his vest pocket and look at the time. I noticed 'cause I'd never seen him do that before. I noticed 'cause he carried a cheap watch. Didn't seem right to me that a lawyer like him would carry just a nickel-plated watch."

"You were asked if he could have taken a knife from one of the drawers."

"I answered that. He could have. I didn't see him do it, but he could have. And gone upstairs and stabbed that man."

10

Leaving the kitchen, the First Lady took the elevator to the second floor, operating it herself.

Reaching her bedroom, she found her signal light blinking. She had a telephone call. At half past one in the morning.

"Ma'am," said the operator. "You have a call from Lieutenant Kennelly, D.C. police. This is the number."

"Call it for me, please," said Mrs. Roosevelt.

The telephone was answered, not by D.C. police headquarters or by Kennelly, but by a hostile-voiced woman.

"A call for Lieutenant Kennelly," said the operator.

"Yeah. Hang on."

After much yelling through halls, Kennelly came on the line. "Mrs. R.? Sorry to call at this time of night, but—"

"Don't be sorry. What's going on?"

"I'm at Margaret Dempsey's boarding house," said

Kennelly. "Everything's in one hell of an uproar here. Somebody has tried to kill her."

"Is she hurt?"

"Fortunately, no."

"I should like to come there."

"Oh, Mrs. Roosevelt, you—"

"Please be so good as to give me the address," she said.

Twenty minutes later the First Lady arrived at the boarding house. She had driven her own blue Buick and parked it behind a police patrol car. The uniformed officers had been alerted to expect her, and one of them met her and led her toward the house.

The officer, a sergeant, had apparently been detailed specifically to wait for her. As they walked along the sidewalk, he gestured emphatically to the officers on the porch, and they moved to clear away the small, curious crowd that had gathered to watch the police operation.

She could see as they climbed to the porch and entered the house that Lieutenant Kennelly had made a point of preserving her anonymity. Obviously, even the police officers themselves did not know who the tall woman was. The residents of the house were kept well back.

Kennelly met her just inside the front door and led her up the front stairs.

"Odd damned thing," he said. "She was in the bathroom, and someone fired five shots through the bathroom door. And he missed her."

The second floor of the boarding house offered four rooms for residents. Margaret Dempsey's front bedroom was the room of choice. Not only was it by far the largest; it was the only room with a private bath off of it, as Kennelly explained. The other residents shared the main bathroom, toward the rear of the house.

The young woman sat on her bed, attended by a uniformed policewoman and by a solicitous man. She was in an obvious state of shock. The bullet-shattered bathroom door was ample evidence of why.

Margaret Dempsey looked up but seemed not to recognize Mrs. Roosevelt.

Kennelly opened the bathroom door. The room was actually very small, hardly larger than a walk-in clothes closet. Still, it was nicely appointed, with a floor and walls of white tile and a toilet, a basin, and a bathtub, tidy and serviceable. The young woman's assembled personal things—brushes, comb, cosmetics, and so on—had made it all the more attractive.

But all was ruined by the bullets that had torn through the door, smashed the white tiles, wrecked the basin and the toilet, and dented the bathtub. The cracked toilet had spewed water until someone had finally thought to turn it off, and the floor was flooded. Debris lay in the water: bits of tile, powdered grouting and plaster, a shattered jar of cold cream.

"How did she survive?" asked Mrs. Roosevelt.

"Damned good question," said Kennelly. "I tried to ask her, but she's hysterical.

"Maybe she would talk with me."

"Maybe."

Margaret Dempsey looked up from her bed, into the face of the First Lady and showed now that she knew her.

The man with her was a physician, and he explained to Mrs. Roosevelt that he had given Margaret a sedative that so far the young woman had fought. He could, he said, increase the dosage soon, to give her a night's sleep. He had not done so only because he suspected more people wanted to talk to her before she became entirely incapable of answering questions.

"Miss Dempsey . . . Do you know me?"

"Mrs. Roosevelt . . ."

"Yes. I am so pleased that you have survived this vicious attack. You are under police protection now, you know."

Margaret Dempsey nodded. She wore a frayed terry-cloth bathrobe: white with faint red, green, yellow stripes. It hung open well down into the cleavage of her generous breasts.

"I know you have told what happened, probably more than once," said the First Lady softly, leaning down to speak directly to the young woman. "Would you mind telling it once more, to me? I— I can hear it woman-to-woman, maybe with more sympathy than you have had from the police."

Margaret Dempsey looked up into the face of the First Lady, and she sobbed. "Oh, Mrs. Roosevelt!" she wept. "I can't believe *you* would come . . ."

"Of course I would come, child," said the First Lady with pronounced sympathy. "Did you imagine I wouldn't, once I heard of what happened? Of course I . . . And I hate to ask you to tell the story again. But—"

"I woke in the middle of the night, Mrs. Roosevelt. I am not sure what time it was. My alarm clock is there—" She pointed at a great old ticking clock. "—but in the dark I didn't see what time it was . . . and didn't care, really. I needed to go to the bathroom. I have lived here long enough that I can find the door in the dark, but

I need the light when I am in the bathroom, and I pulled the chain over the basin and switched on the light."

"Yes."

"I was sitting on the toilet . . . half asleep. Quite naked. I live alone in this room and don't wear a nightgown. And—And . . ."

"My dear . . ."

"BANG! I mean, a bullet crashed through the door and hit one of the tiles above the tub. I mean . . . It was *awful*! *A bullet*! I . . . I don't know—I don't know . . ."

Mrs. Roosevelt put her hand on the girl's. "But what did you *do*, my dear? You survived—"

Margaret Dempsey shook her head. "I . . . I didn't know what to do! But— Some kind of instinct. I threw myself off the toilet and into the bathtub. And . . . And more bullets came. They— I lay down as flat as I could in the bottom of the tub. I heard the bullets. I felt them! One, at least, hit the tub and shook it. And I . . . I just lay there. Trembling . . ."

"This is exactly how she told it to me," said Kennelly. "Whoever was firing at her . . . Well, he emptied his pistol, I'd guess. She was screaming. All over the house people were screaming. Headquarters got five calls. The neighbors called."

"Did anyone see the person who did this?" asked the First Lady.

Margaret Dempsey shook her head.

"Nobody saw him, apparently," said Kennelly. "People were afraid to come out of their rooms for a minute or so. They heard him banging around and then—"

"How did he get out of the house?" asked Mrs. Roosevelt.

"Down the fire escape, apparently," said Kennelly.

"The door at the end of the hall goes out to the fire escape. That door was open when people first looked out from their bedrooms."

Mrs. Roosevelt turned and stared hard into the bathroom. She glanced into the face of Kennelly. Then she said to Margaret Dempsey, "Do you have any idea who did this? Or why?"

The young woman sighed. "I can only think it was a friend of Shondor Jack," she said. "I can't think of anyone else who would want to . . . would want to kill me."

"And why would a friend of Shondor Jack want to kill you?"

Margaret Dempsey shook her head. She seemed to struggle for breath. "Let me talk to you about it tomorrow," she whispered. "I guess the doctor's injection is beginning to take effect. A few hours . . ." She shook her head. "It won't make any difference. Not anyway as long as I have some protection."

"You'll have it," said Kennelly.

The policewoman helped her to lie back on her pillows, and Margaret Dempsey closed her eyes.

"What do you think, Lieutenant?" asked Mrs. Roosevelt when she and Kennelly were out on the street.

"I met a gambler tonight, a bookie," said Kennelly. "He took Shondor Jack's action. Shondor was into him for two hundred dollars and wanted more credit. He kept telling the man he was on the verge of a 'big score.' I'd like to know what the big score was. I can't help wonder if both Asman and Miss Dempsey didn't have something to do with it."

"Like—?"

"Like they were his partners in something, or they were spoiling a deal for him."

"But Shondor Jack is dead. He was the first one killed."

"Guy like him . . . Who knows who else he had workin' on this 'big score'? I don't know. I wish I did."

"Even so," she said, "what about it would motivate someone to murder Mr. Asman and attempt to murder Miss Dempsey? If the score has been . . . How shall we say? If it has been frustrated—prevented, is perhaps the better word—then the only motive has to be revenge. Or—"

"Or maybe Asman or Miss Dempsey had information that—"

"Not likely," Mrs. Roosevelt interrupted. "If someone wanted information, he would hardly have shot Mr. Asman to death in an alley and attempted to kill Miss Dempsey. If the motive involves information, I should think it more likely someone is trying to *prevent* the disclosure of information."

"Well . . . Chris Asman is not going to disclose it," said Kennelly.

"No. That is for certain."

They stood in the pale glow of a street light hanging above the nearby intersection. In that light the First Lady could see Ed Kennelly's face break into an amused grin. "Risking being accused of sharing what I called class prejudice," he said, "I guess what happened in that boarding house tonight shifts a lot of attention away from Senator Fisher and Congressman Metcalf."

Mrs. Roosevelt smiled. "Oh, I'm not so sure," she said. "Maybe to the contrary, actually. If people of their social class—and, to be perfectly frank with you, Lieutenant,

I'm not sure either of them shares the graces of the class I believe we were talking about earlier . . . Anyway, if people of their social class are supposed to be clever—Well, if I were one of them and guilty of murdering Mr. Asman and were trying to confuse the investigation . . . Do you follow?"

"You would take some shots at Miss Dempsey?" asked Kennelly skeptically.

"Lieutenant . . ." she said. "Does it not occur to you that there is something odd about that attempt on the life of Miss Dempsey? Why did her assailant stand outside her bathroom and fire shots through the closed door when, just as easily, he could have jerked the door open and fired one deadly shot into her defenseless body?"

Ed Kennelly turned his eyes away and for a long moment stared at the street light. Flakes of snow had just begun to glitter in the weak light. "Mrs. R.," he said. "The implications in what you just said . . . Well, hell, Ma'am. You just opened the biggest can of worms I've had to think about in a long time."

"'A can of worms.' Well, that is not the turn of phrase that came to my mind, but I assume it means we are faced with a confusing variety of possibilities."

"I can think of fifty," said Kennelly wryly.

"Would you like to sit down somewhere over a cup of coffee and review some of them?" she asked. "Of course . . . it is . . . What is it?"

"Nearly three A.M.," he said.

"Ahh. Well. Too late to ask you to—"

"The night's shot," he said. "I won't sleep now. Why not have a cup of coffee and talk, while the mind is fresh on the problem? That is, if you—"

"I imagine you know an all-night diner where—"

"Oh, I do, Ma'am. I definitely do."

It *was* a diner, a long, narrow little building with a long counter faced by stools and with a few booths along the front windows. At three in the morning, two men sat on stools hunched over big, heavy coffee mugs, intent on inhaling the steam as much as on drinking coffee. A Secret Service agent, but not Stan Szczygiel, had arrived in response to a suggestion from District police headquarters and sat inconspicuously sipping coffee. If the counter man recognized the First Lady, it raised no reaction from him—as if it were perfectly ordinary for the wife of the President to pop in not long before dawn. She ordered coffee. Kennelly, who was hungry, asked for cherry pie with ice cream, as well.

For a minute or so they did not launch their analysis of the new developments in their mystery, and during that minute Ed Kennelly sat and looked at this woman, Eleanor Roosevelt, wife of the President of the United States. He had worked with her before and had learned to respect her mind. Now, sitting across the table from her in an all-night diner, he realized that this woman was a *woman*, goddammit, and one who was unfairly abused by people who didn't see her closely enough to appreciate her. The story of Eleanor Roosevelt was that she was unattractive, a gawky, too-tall, buck-toothed woman her husband probably barely tolerated. Some people wondered how Franklin Roosevelt, himself handsome and debonair—and still so in spite of infantile paralysis—could ever have chosen this ungainly distant cousin for a wife. Ed Kennelly was an Irishman and in his own opinion a good judge of horses and women. He stared for a very long moment at Eleanor Roosevelt and decided she was . . . Well, if she were not the wife of the President of the United States, he would suggest to her a closer relationship—and would congratulate himself on his ability to see in her the qualities her husband was lucky to have appreciated, too. If she had been someone else, he would, at his age and hers, not have been embarrassed to squire *this* colleen to a dance of the Emerald Society.

"Can you imagine?" she asked—her thoughts in a strange way paralleling his—"Can you imagine how much it means to me, a woman in my situation, to have the privilege to sit here at this hour in this place and face the problems we do?"

"My dear lady—"

"The problems I face daily are challenging enough. There is never enough time to confront them all. I am committed—"

"To making this a better country," Kennelly interrupted.

"Yes, but— A professor once said to me . . . A professor who joined my husband in the so-called Brain Trust . . . He said, 'You know, it is one thing to sit in the shade and dust of a university campus and plot our solutions to major problems; but it is another thing altogether to plot out a solution and then have to put it into practical application. That is not an easy bridge to cross.' I have interfered in criminal investigations, when my participation—"

"Was always valued, always needed," said Kennelly.

"Uhmm. Not necessarily. But you see— Justice in the abstract and justice in its harsh reality should not be so far apart. Theorizing about how to help the farmers, and facing their problems on their land . . . two different things. I so much welcome the chance to see real problems in real settings. That's why I worked on the Athurdale community."

Kennelly understood that she was talking about a social project she had personally sponsored in West Virginia, to give deprived people decent homes and a chance to earn their own way in the world, free of public charity. It had not been one-hundred-per cent successful, but it represented a practical, non-theoretical approach to solving a dramatically perceived problem.

Ed Kennelly decided, a little abruptly, that he was committed to this woman. He would never approach her more closely than he was right now, but that was enough. He would always be glad he had known her.

Conscious that their thoughts ran along lines that were too close and that it would be well to separate them, Ed Kennelly grinned and looked around and said: "Nothing in this whole weird world smells like a diner at three A.M."

"I have not visited them as often as I could wish," she said.

"Ah, but you should. You must. Here is America. One part of it."

"Yes, I know. But who fired five shots through Miss Dempsey's bathroom door? And why?"

"Quick answer? I don't know."

"I want to look into something as quickly as possible," said Mrs. Roosevelt. "Professor Frankfurter says no Mr. Christian Asman ever attended Harvard law. His letters of recommendation say he did."

"Forgive me about something," said Kennelly. "Class prejudice again . . . Or whatever it is. I just can't believe Margaret Dempsey is anything but a victim in this whole problem. Somebody fired shots at her—"

"Lieutenant . . . Let's face something. Whoever fired five shots through Miss Dempsey's bathroom door did not mean to kill her. If he had meant to do so, he *would* have killed her. We are looking at a charade."

"By whom?" he asked.

"Before we turn to that question, let's satisfy ourselves that it *is* a charade. I wouldn't want to be wrong on the point. But consider—In the first place, is it not an odd coincidence that Miss Dempsey's would-be killer happened to arrive during the very few minutes of the entire night during which Miss Dempsey was not in bed but was in the bathroom? If he had entered her room and found her in bed, he could have shot her perfectly easily. Instead, he saw light in the bathroom and fired through the door. As I asked before, why on earth did he not simply open the door? And then, firing five shots into a tiny bathroom, he somehow failed to hit Miss Dempsey even once."

"Well . . . the steel bathtub did stop one bullet," said Kennelly.

Mrs. Roosevelt clasped her coffee mug in both hands. It was instinctive in most people to handle a big heavy mug that way. The heat came through to her fingers. She did not lift the mug, just sat for a moment, pondering. Finally, she said—"

"I do not want to be unfair to Miss Dempsey. You've said you can't believe she is anything but a victim. I'd like to think so, too. But the facts— Lieutenant, I simply can't believe Margaret Dempsey was in that bathroom when the shots were fired."

"Then where was she?"

"I don't know. Still in bed. Under the bed. Here's a possibility: She heard the gunman opening her door. She rolled off the bed and under it. He came in, saw she was not in bed, saw the light in the bathroom, and fired through the door."

Kennelly smiled wanly. "That theory asks more questions than it answers."

Mrs. Roosevelt nodded. "Chief among which is, why would she then tell us she was in the bathroom?"

"I can think of one possible answer," said Kennelly. "She was in panic, then shock. She saw the bathroom shattered by bullets. She knew the gunman meant to kill her in there. Maybe she imagines she was, in fact, in there. I've seen reactions like that, in people who've survived something horrible."

"Not a very likely explanation, however," remarked the First Lady.

"Thinking along those lines, let me suggest an explanation as to why the gunman fired through the bathroom door. Once again, panic. Suppose the guy had broken into the boarding house, is scared out of his wits, reaches the second floor, opens the girl's bedroom door, and in the light from the hall he sees she's not in bed—because, like you suggested, she heard him just in time and rolled out and under; or maybe, like she said, she's gone in the bathroom. He sees the light in the bathroom. He'd planned on firing a shot in the dark, or in dim light, into a sleeping girl. Now he has to open the door, see her in the light, look her in the face as he kills her. Maybe he can't bring himself to do that. So he empties his revolver through the door. And runs."

"My scenario and yours are about equally valid," said Mrs. Roosevelt glumly.

"I can think of one way to strengthen it," he said. "If the gunman was an amateur, a guy who'd never done anything like this before, then there's at least a little sense in my idea."

"Are you thinking about Senator Fisher and Congressman Metcalf?" she asked.

"Well, you said either one of them had a motive—a motive, that is, if one of them killed Asman. The idea is a little farfetched, but—"

"To confuse the investigation, to suggest that Mr. Asman and Miss Dempsey were co-conspirators in some scheme that . . ." She smiled. "Yes, it is a bit farfetched. It would become a little less farfetched if one or both of them cannot account for his whereabouts at the time when the shots were fired into that bathroom. Neither of them can account for his whereabouts when Mr. Asman was killed. Would it not be a suggestive coincidence that one of them cannot account for his whereabouts at the time of *either* shooting?"

"I suppose we have to find out," said Kennelly without enthusiasm.

"With some subtlety, if possible," said Mrs. Roosevelt.

Stan Szczygiel had had a decent night's sleep. At ten in the morning he had as yet heard nothing from Ed Kennelly or the First Lady, and he was busy checking out the validity of an idea that had occurred to him.

A little before ten he had left the White House and walked around to the gate on East Executive Avenue. There he joined the crowd that was lined up for the daily tour of the public rooms. He was near the end of the line, but that was all right; it was where he wanted to be. Men, women, and children stood patiently in line, many of them stamping their feet quietly. A dusting of snow had fallen overnight, and their shuffling and stamping cleared the sidewalk.

The gate opened promptly at ten, and a guide welcomed the crowd to the White House. Szczygiel was amused by his wooden spiel:

"This pavilion, which you're walking through now, was not a part of the original White House but was built during the administration of President Thomas Jefferson. It will probably be torn down soon, since there's a plan afoot to build an East Wing on the White House, one that it is said will complement the existing West Wing, or Executive Wing, that was built during the presidency of Theodore Roosevelt and houses the famous Oval Office and the other executive offices of the President and his staff. We will enter the White House on the ground floor, which houses a library and some storage rooms but is given over chiefly to the kitchens and pantries, the office of the housekeeper, and a suite of rooms for the White House physician, including a clinic where he can examine patients. The state rooms, which are far more interesting, are up one flight, and we will go up there as soon as you've had a chance to take off your coats if you want to and get a little more comfortable."

The crowd on this damp and chilly February morning did not exceed forty people, but all of them were conspicuously curious and excited; many of them kept a sharp eye in all directions, as if they expected to catch a glimpse of the President or maybe of Mrs. Roosevelt. Most of them probably imagined that the First Family lived in the beautiful state rooms they were about to see.

Few understood that the Roosevelt family resided only in a modest private suite on the second floor.

The guide led the crowd up the broad stairway to the long Cross Hall, then left, into the East Room. After he had described how the bodies of presidents had lain in state there, the guide took the visitors to see the Blue Room, the Red Room, the Green Room, and the State Dining Room.

Though the steamboat-gothic decorations and furnishings installed in the late 19th century had been for the most part removed, many visitors were shocked by the generally shabby state of the White House. Simply said, the state rooms resembled a high-class secondhand store, with rooms a-jumble with whatever had accrued over the decades, some of it ugly and some of it cheap. Historians and others had urged the Congress to appoint a commission and appropriate money to restore the décor of the mansion to what it had been under Jefferson and Madison; but the legislators had been reluctant to spend.

But décor did not concern Stan Szczygiel. He had come along on the guided tour to see something else.

And see it he did. The tour group straggled through the rooms, some staying behind a little to have a better look at something. Uniformed police looked into each room after the tour moved on, to make sure everyone was out; but their look was perfunctory, nothing that would have prevented a determined tourist from abandoning the group and remaining behind in the White House.

Which was just the point.

On the ground floor especially there were rooms not often used. A tourist abandoning the group could slip into one of those and wait . . .

After the tour group was gone, Szczygiel questioned the guide.

"You don't count them?"

"No. I've always said we should have tickets, with numbers printed on so we'd know how many came in. We could make them surrender those tickets on their way out. We could— Oh, we could do a lot of things. But we don't. And for one reason, just one: It's always been done this way. Hell, Mr. Szczygiel, I can remember the day when any citizen could walk into the White House and wander arond looking for himself, didn't need a guide. The idea is: You can walk into the Capitol, so why can't you walk into the White House? Making them come through on guided tours caused fuss enough."

Szczygiel thanked the man. Now he knew how Shondor Jack had entered the White House.

Speaking to Mrs. Roosevelt a little later, he expanded on the idea. "It's unlikely he stayed hidden somewhere all day and into the evening. He was an experienced burglar. My guess is, he entered the house with the tour, broke off on the ground floor, went into some room and unlocked a window. He rejoined the tour and left when the crowd left, then came back to that window after dark."

"And it was easy enough for him to pick up the mimeographed telephone list, either in the morning or in the evening," she said.

"Right."

Ed Kennelly had arrived. "While I was trying to get an hour or two of shut-eye," he said, "another question came to my mind. How did the gunman last night know which room was Margaret Dempsey's?"

"Three possible answers to a question that came to

me, too," said the First Lady. "One, he had been in the room before. Two, he had dropped off Miss Dempsey after being with her during the evening and watched the house to see which bedroom light came on. Three, he had followed her and then watched."

"I need to know what you are talking about," said Szczygiel. "In the meantime, I have one more bit of information for you. Asman had two letters of recommendation. One was from a New York lawyer named Jonathan Merrill. The other was from a New York lawyer named Melvin Shapiro. You asked me to locate Shapiro."

"Yes," said Mrs. Roosevelt. "Have you found him?"

"Not yet," said Szczygiel. "But I know where he is. He's in Washington for a hearing before the Securities and Exchange Commission. I left word at his hotel and at the Commission office that he is to telephone me as soon as possible."

"Let us hope," said the First Lady, "that he proves more candid and helpful than Mr. Merrill has been."

11

"You might do well to immerse yourself a little more in Washington gossip," said the President to Mrs. Roosevelt.

They sat in the Oval Office, where he was taking his lunch from a tray on his desk: a ham sandwich, an apple, and coffee.

"I never really had the time or interest," she said.

"Gossip fuels a lot of this town's machinery," he said. "Not everybody is moved by ideals and ideas."

"Precisely what gossip do you have in mind, Franklin?" she asked.

"The charming daughter of the senior senator from Arkansas," he said. "She is well known to Alice: indeed, one of Alice's favorite topics of conversation. Alice phoned when she read of Asman's death. You ought to talk to her, Babs. You and Alice detest each other so much that you will have a charming conversation. I firmly recommend you go see her. You will enjoy the afternoon."

"I doubt it," said Mrs. Roosevelt sharply.

Nevertheless, she telephoned Alice Roosevelt Longworth, who instantly invited her to tea.

Alice Roosevelt Longworth was the daughter of President Theodore Roosevelt. Her White House wedding to Congressman Nicholas Longworth had been *the* social event of the year 1906. After her husband's death she had returned to Washington from Cincinnati and lived there as an authentic grande dame, writing a vinegary Republican newspaper column. She was beloved of editors, who gratefully published her every pithy comment on public figures who included her distant cousin, the current President of the United States. The public figures cringed. (It was Alice who, years later, actually damaged the public image of Thomas E. Dewey with her remark that he looked like the little bridegroom on a wedding cake.)

Alice presided over a salon. It was precisely the sort of milieu in which her cousin Eleanor functioned worst.

But for this tea, she had not summoned the habitués of her salon. She received Mrs. Roosevelt alone in her living room, in the midst of her extensive collection of mementoes and surrounded by enough fresh-cut flowers to have graced a major funeral.

Alice was, of course, a formidable lady, with an air of being something from the past, though in fact Mrs. Longworth was the same age as the First Lady. In fact, Alice had been a bridesmaid at Eleanor's wedding.

"The murder of Christian Asman is a fascinating development," said Mrs. Longworth. "If ever there is a funeral—and I gather there is not going to be—the female mourners should be an interesting group. For a man who spent only a year or so in Washington, he cut a wide swath."

"He did indeed," said Mrs. Roosevelt, "and very likely committed a murder."

"Oh, you are talking about the business of Djaković. I am doing you a favor, Eleanor, and am not talking about that."

"It would be embarrassing to have to admit that a murder took place in one of the state rooms of the White House," said Mrs. Roosevelt.

"Are you aware," asked Mrs. Longworth, "that *two* murders happened in the White House while Father was presiding? He hushed them. But they happened. Ah, the dear old White House has a dark history."

"An unfortunate dark *side* to a brilliant history," said Mrs. Roosevelt.

"That's the difference between us, Eleanor. You see the good as normal and perceive the bad as a minor aberration. I perceive the bad as normal and the good as aberrational."

Alice Longworth lit a cigarette. She remained the tall, slender strikingly beautiful woman she had always been, though she was now fifty-three years old. She performed even the act of lighting a cigarette with a grace that people remarked on. Mrs. Roosevelt would not deny that she had long envied Alice her appearance and style—though she would not have wanted her character.

"Franklin says you have a great deal of information about Senator and Miss Fisher."

"Oh . . . Gossip. Lots of Gossip. But, the White House, Eleanor. We should not be surprised if dark deeds are done there. It is a place where forceful and ambitious men congregate. Who knows what they are capable of doing? I would like some time to write a *scandal* history of the White House. Why should we suppose ghosts don't walk the corridors of the White House, as they are supposed to do at Windsor Castle or the Palace of Versailles or the Hermitage? In a century—" She laughed. "What kind of people would we be if our statesmen didn't have skeletons in their closets?"

"I am not naive, Alice."

Mrs. Longworth laughed gently. "Well, such is your reputation. But— What is it you want to talk about? Fisher?"

"Franklin said—"

"Yes," said Mrs. Longworth crisply. "Where the hell's the tea? Abigail!"

They waited while a young woman brought the tea and tea things. Mrs. Longworth poured: again with a style that cloyed and yet survived.

"Fisher . . ." she said. "Senator Fisher. And his daughter. Fisher came here from Arkansas in nineteen twenty-three. With a hypochondriac wife and his daughter, then thirteen. Now, tell me, Eleanor, does *anybody* come from Arkansas? I mean, after all! *Arkansas!* I suppose Fisher was Arkansas nobility. He was a professional gambler, the story is. And a bootlegger. Arkansas aristocracy. The daughter . . . Eleanor! What do you want to know?"

"She was engaged to marry Congressman Vernon Metcalf of Ohio. She—"

"Metcalf! Her *father* wanted her to marry Metcalf. My God Eleanor, you should know how politics runs in Ohio! The Harding Gang . . . But even worse in Cleveland! Eleanor! Everything in Cleveland is for sale! To the best bidder! Metcalf is a foundry owner. That is, he inherited his father's foundry. He bought himself a seat on the Cleveland City Council, cheap. I mean, you can buy a seat on the Cleveland City Council for three hundred dollars. He liked politics. He bought his seat in the House of Representatives! It cost more than three hundred bucks, but— Eleanor! *Cleveland*, for God's sake!"

"Cincinnati, dear?" asked Mrs. Roosevelt, referring to the city of origin of Nicholas Longworth.

Alice Roosevelt Longworth sipped tea. "The political hero of Cincinnati, Eleanor, is Adolf Hitler, where he is as well regarded as is, say, the late Huey Long, another Cincinnati hero. In Cleveland the hero is Benito Mussolini. Also, they rather favor Joseph Stalin in Cleveland. In Cincinnati, Genghis Khan. But—Joan Fisher."

"Yes, please. Let's do talk about Miss Fisher."

She grew up in Washington. She saw the worst of it, never the best. Metcalf was by no means her first affair. Her father used her. Eleanor, he offered the girl to senators to promote—"

"Alice!"

Alice Roosevelt Longworth shrugged. "The standards that govern your life and mine, your husband's, my father's . . . don't count with these . . . don't always count in Arkansas and Ohio. Or in California. Eleanor . . . Joan Fisher has lived a difficult life. She is no innocent girl. She has an attractive style, I know. She has observed and learned. But—"

"What do you know about Christian Asman?" asked Mrs. Roosevelt.

"More than that miserable little man deserves that I should know," said Mrs. Longworth. "He was responsible for the destruction of the engagement between Joan Fisher and Vernon Metcalf. For whatever sins he must answer before God, that achievement will go a long way toward earning him an apartment in heaven."

"Alice . . . Where do I look for the murderer of Christian Asman?"

"Senator Fisher," said Mrs. Longworth. "He wanted a politically advantageous marriage for Joan—and for reasons I don't entirely understand, he saw advantage in the match with Metcalf. You would have to turn over rocks and scrape away the worms to figure that one out. Metcalf could also have done it. He does not take public humiliation easily. The relationship between Joan and Asman *humiliated* him—among knowledgeable people."

"Very well," said the First Lady. "Then where do I look for the murderer of Shondor Jack?"

"Under the rocks," said Mrs. Longworth. "There is something very slimy in a wide range of relationships—Asman to Jack, Jack to Metcalf, Metcalf to Fisher . . . The Cleveland connection, Eleanor. Pursue the Cleveland connection."

Mrs. Roosevelt smiled. "Does it seem strange to you, Alice, that you and I should be sitting here, in nineteen thirty-seven, absorbed in the doings of the kind of people we are talking about? Not the sort of thing people like us are supposed to do, huh?"

Alice Roosevelt Longworth smiled. "Politics, Eleanor," she said quietly. "Franklin had to associate with Al Smith. Why should either of us be surprised to find ourselves looking into the doings of criminals? Their kind are a part of democracy, are they not? I mean, crooks vote. Let's hope they don't make up a majority, but they do vote. And so do illiterates. And—"

"Enough, Alice," said Mrs. Roosevelt. "I can guess who you are about to mention next. I . . . I am grateful to you. Do you really think Joan Fisher—?"

"Joan Fisher," said Alice Roosevelt Longworth, "has in essence—though not of course in blunt reality—been sold in prostitution. If she is not bitter— Well, let us imagine she *is* bitter. Extremely. And she might like to harm her father. Don't forget that, Eleanor. She has ample motive to wish her father ill."

With all that on her mind, Mrs. Roosevelt returned to the White House very late in the afternoon.

She found waiting on her desk a note from Lieutenant Kennelly:

> Ballistics tests were performed on the bullets retrieved from Margaret Dempsey's bathroom. Because the slugs hit hard objects like bathroom stuff and tiles, they are all pretty well crushed down. Even so, it looks like the bullets from the revolver that fired those shots might match the slugs taken from the body of Asman. Interesting development, don't you think?

She would have liked very much to give her attention to that and other problems; but she was scheduled that Tuesday evening to attend the opening of an art exhibit. A selection of the works of Georgia O'Keeffe was opening at the Corcoran Gallery. She herself had encouraged the Corcoran to hold an exhibition of the works of Miss O'Keeffe (that is, Mrs. Alfred Stieglitz), and she could hardly avoid attending the opening.

The works exhibited that evening were, for the most part, Miss O'Keeffe's giant flower paintings: immensely enlarged images of blossoms, in vivid color and full detail. A few paintings represented a new departure for the famous artist. Near her new home in New Mexico, she had found the sun-bleached bones of cattle, lying abandoned and ignored on the desert floor. To her, those bones dramatized the barren beauty of a part of the country most Americans never saw, or, if they saw it, never appreciated. She had painted dramatic images of cattle skulls in strong basic colors, mostly red, white, and blue. The paintings were controversial—as anything unfamiliar invariably is—but attracted and held attention as even her huge flowers did not.

Georgia O'Keeffe was almost as well known for her husband's photographic portraits of her as she was for her painting, but this was her evening, and Mrs. Roosevelt was pleased to be a part of an event in which a woman was exhibiting her own work, apart from the achievements of her husband.

While Mrs. Roosevelt stood beside the artist, an imposing woman with formidable black eyebrows, a reporter asked the meaning of a huge painting of a morning glory.

"It's just a great big damned flower, can't you see?" said Georgia O'Keeffe, who then turned and laughed with Mrs. Roosevelt.

The night Asman was killed, Kennelly had sent an officer to the victim's apartment building with orders that no one was to enter Asman's flat and that the door was to be kept locked. The officer put a seal on it. Kennelly wanted to go back and take a closer look at the flat, but it hadn't been a high priority with him. He didn't expect to find anything much there. Besides, with the incident in the Dempsey girl's room and everything else that had been happening, he had not found time to return until today.

The seal was broken. Not just broken, it was gone. The door was locked, but someone had entered the apartment.

Looking around to be sure he was not seen, Kennelly opened the door with his skeleton key and went in.

The place looked very much the way it had on Friday. It had not been searched, ransacked.

Kennelly went into the bedroom. He would take the gold watch and the photograph of the child, as evidence. He opened the dresser drawer where he had found them. They were gone.

Now he began to look around more closely. In the bathroom the cosmetics were gone from the cabinet. In the living room the ashtray that had contained the ashes and butts of both cigars and cigarettes now had only three cigar butts. He checked the trash baskets in the living room, kitchen, and bedroom. No ashes or butts. Whoever had cleaned the ashtray had probably flushed the contents down the toilet. The dishes in the sink had been washed and put away in the cabinet.

For a minute or two Kennelly stood in the middle of the living room, staring, thinking. Okay. Asman had dumped Stormy Skye's cigarette butts out of the ashtray before he brought Joan Fisher here Friday night. Maybe he had even cleaned up the kitchen. Maybe he had hidden the cosmetics in the bathroom.

But where was the watch and the picture of the child?

And who had broken the police seal on the door to this flat?

Kennelly spent ten minutes searching for the cosmetics. He went through the drawers, turning over Asman's socks, underwear, and shirts. He went through the pockets of the clothes hanging in the bedroom closet.

Something odd. He found nothing in the pockets, but examining Asman's suits he discovered that all the labels had been cut out.

Okay. That hooked it. Christian Asman was not Christian Asman. Then who the devil had he been?

The President was holding a press conference. He always enjoyed these occasions; they afforded him an opportunity to do what he did best: bring the force of his personality to bear to persuade people to do what he wanted them to do—and in the case of press conferences, to persuade reporters to report the news *his* way.

The conferences were held in the Oval Office, with reporters standing around the President's desk. They stood, listened, and scribbled notes. They could paraphrase what the President said, but were not to quote him directly. When the President wanted to be quoted directly, he handed out a statement. This had been the practice of every President since American chief executives began to talk directly to reporters.

This morning the group was assembled to hear the President tell them how things were going with his judicial-reform package.

"I understand," he said, "how some traditionalists find fault with my proposal to reform the nation's judiciary, but I am certain that as the facts come out and reasoned discussion replaces angry first reaction, we will secure passage of this vital legislation."

A reporter asked, "Are you disturbed, Mr. President, by the almost unanimous editorial opposition you have had from the nation's newspapers?"

The President grinned. "I would say I am disappointed. I am not disturbed. I know you fellows report the facts accurately, but I also know that your publishers don't like me and don't like this plan and will do all they can to defeat it."

"Mr. President, you have indicated you want to increase the number of justices on the Supreme Court because the Court is over-burdened with work. But Chief Justice Charles Evans Hughes has made a statement this morning that says the Court is not overworked and doesn't need extra justices."

The President grinned again. "If you were the chief and had reached his age, and if somebody asked you if you were overworked, what would *you* say? Of course the older justices don't want to admit the burden has become too great for them."

Several of the reporters noticed that the President didn't like the answer he had given. He had been surprised by the Hughes statement, which he was hearing about for the first time, and he wasn't happy.

"Mr. President, a number of organizations have weighed in against your plan."

Now the discussion was back on ground the President liked better. His grin broadened—because now it was genuine—and he lit a Camel and lifted his chin. "The only organization that supports me," he said, "is the organized people of these United States. The Democratic Party. And we're going to win this thing. As I said before, I'm waiting for reasoned discussion to supplant the initial irrational reaction."

Reporters did not remind him that some of his most vocal opposition came from leaders of the Democratic Party.

"I want you to know something," said Kennelly. "We're talking about two murders, with one that's definitely a matter of federal jurisdiction. Holding back information, playing coy, is going to get you in big, deep trouble. I can take you downtown and lock you in a cell, kiddo. You know I can. You've been in jail and know what it's like. Remember? You didn't like it much."

He was talking to Teddy O'Neil, once again in her living room where her canaries sang among the flowers. She offered him a cigarette, but he smoked Luckies and lit one of his own. Teddy was dressed as she had been when he and Szczygiel interviewed her Saturday: in a white nightgown covered by a sheer white peignoir; modest enough, and yet erotic. He could not see her skin, but the outline of her body was quite clear.

"So Rumpelstiltskin's dead," she said, remembering how she had responded when he tossed the name "Asman" at her for the first time. "When I read about that, I wondered if you would come back. What is it you want to know?"

"You told me Shondor Jack tried to muscle you, and you told me he couldn't because you have a man you call your insurance, named 'Deeter.' Well, I've run that nickname through the files, and I've put the word out to a lot of cops, and nobody ever heard of this fellow Deeter."

"I can't help it if the guy doesn't have a criminal record."

"I want to talk to this Deeter," said Kennelly. "Maybe *he* killed Shondor Jack. You've suggested a motive. Where do I find him?"

"I . . . don't know. Not right off."

"He's your protection," Kennelly persisted. "How do you get in touch with him?"

"I leave word around that I need to see him."

"You leave word where?"

"Bartenders."

"Name one. Name two or three."

"I don't know bartenders by name."

"Name the bars."

"Hey, I . . . I—"

"Want to start telling the truth? Or you want to go down to headquarters?"

She crushed her cigarette in a glass ashtray. "Okay. But I had nothin' to do with either one of them getting killed. *Nothing.* I mean it."

"You'd be more convincing on that point if you'd told the truth last week," he said coldly.

She scratched a match and lit another Wings. "Once a guy like Shondor Jack gets his hooks in you, there's no way to get away from him. Yeah, I ran away from him when he was in jail in Cleveland, ran away for good when they took him to the pen. But he never got to the pen, as you know. I never went back to Cleveland, but I didn't lose touch with everybody there, not absolutely. Some people in Cleveland knew I was in Washington. So Shondor Jack shows up. I said a guy called Deeter muscled him. I wish it was so. There was only one way I could have got away from that son of a bitch, and that way was to kill him. Which I couldn't do. He took half what I made. Half what he *thought* I made. He didn't know how good I am."

"Asman . . ." said Kennelly.

She shook her head. "There's no such guy. The guy you call Asman is Preston. He was a Cleveland lawyer."

"So what was your connection with Asman-Preston?"

"He got me out of jail in Cleveland. A couple of times. He knew I was here. When he came to Washington, he looked me up. That's how Shondor found out Preston was in Washington. I got mad because Preston insisted he wanted free what I sell for a living. He pushed me pretty hard about it, and I told Shondor."

"Was there a past connection between Asman-Preston and Shondor Jack?"

"You better believe it," said Teddy. "John Preston was Shondor's lawyer. He's the one that got Shondor off on that murder charge."

While Ed Kennelly was interviewing Teddy O'Neil, and Mrs. Roosevelt was taking tea with Alice Roosevelt Longworth, Stan Szczygiel had been trying, with as much subtlety as possible, to discover whether or not Senator Fisher and Representative Metcalf had alibis for last night. Could either of them have fired the shots into Margaret Dempsey's bathroom?

Szczygiel and Kennelly came to the First Lady's office at six thirty.

"The whole damned case has changed a hundred per cent," said Kennelly, anxious to tell what he had learned from Teddy O'Neil. "Asman wasn't Asman. He was a Cleveland lawyer named John Preston. He defended Teddy on morals charges and Djaković on the Murder

One charge. Djaković was Teddy's pimp. Margaret Dempsey was, of course, the key witness at the murder trial, and so had to know Asman was really Preston. So— So . . ."

Mrs. Roosevelt shook her head. "I am not sure this tells us who killed Mr. Djaković and who killed Mr. Asman. Excuse me, but I do not see how it tells us who fired the shots through Miss Dempsey's bathroom door.

Kennelly nodded impatiently as she spoke. "Of course it doesn't," he said. "But now we know what we are dealing with."

"I am not certain it follows logically that we do," said the First Lady. "Please tell us, Lieutenant, who you think committed these several crimes, on the basis of his new information."

Kennelly frowned and considered the question for a moment. "The truth is . . . I don't think we know anything for certain until we find out why a lawyer named John Preston was masquerading in Washington under the name Christian Asman."

"And why two reasonably distinguished New York lawyers wrote letters assuring us that they knew Christian Asman and could recommend him," said Mrs. Roosevelt.

"Let me place another call to Melvin Shapiro," said Szczygiel. "He has not returned my call."

While the First Lady and Ed Kennelly waited, Szczygiel put through a telephone call to Shapiro's hotel. He spoke with someone for a moment, then hung up.

"He left me a message. He regrets he is so busy, but he will call me as soon as possible, probably tomorrow."

"I can have a couple of cops go pick the son of a bitch

up and bum's rush him over here in handcuffs," said Kennelly.

"Let's don't," said Mrs. Roosevelt. "We want to be as circumspect about this investigation as possible. After all, Shondor Jack was murdered in the Red Room."

Kennelly grunted. "I went back to Asman's—Preston's—apartment. The police seal on the door was broken, and the gold watch and the photograph of the child are missing."

"Missing since his death?" asked Mrs. Roosevelt.

"It's not absolutely impossible he took them away before he was killed Saturday night," said Kennelly. "On the other hand, who broke the seal on the door—which was not put there until after his death?"

"Someone with a key to his door," Szczygiel suggested.

"Well, not necessarily," said Kennelly. "Those locks don't amount to much. I've twice used the simplest possible skeleton key to get in. Depends on what kind of person it was who got in."

Mrs. Roosevelt rose from her desk and walked to the window, where she stood for a moment staring across the Ellipse at the lights on the Washington Monument. For a brief moment she felt an over-powering sense of bodily weariness. She was tempted to walk out into the Sitting Hall where the President was now presiding over his cocktail hour. She was tempted to take a glass of sherry, which might make her sleepy, and then she might want to go to bed early.

But she did not succumb to those temptations. "Mr. Szczygiel," she said, "may I hope you learned that neither Senator Fisher nor Congressman Metcalf could possibly have fired the shots at Miss Dempsey? Because they were at dinner, drunk in some bar surrounded by witnesses, or— Dare I hope?"

"I regret, my dear lady, that you cannot," said Szczygiel. "So far as I can determine, without directly confronting either of the gentlemen and demanding an answer, Senator Fisher retired last night about eleven, in his own bedroom, and could therefore have easily left his own house, gone to Miss Dempsey's boarding house and fired shots at her, and returned to his bedroom without wife or daughter being the wiser. Representative Metcalf, being a bachelor, could have done it even more easily."

"I wonder," she said, "if Representative Metcalf understood that Mr. Asman was in reality Mr. Preston."

"And Senator Fisher?" asked Szczygiel.

"Oh, I suppose Senator Fisher didn't know," she said. "He is the only major player in this drama who is not from Cleveland."

"Probably the one not capable of killing," said Kennelly.

"A southern senator?" asked Szczygiel. "Not capable of killing? How many lynchings happened in Arkansas last year? Or in Mississippi or Louisiana, the neighboring states? Don't be naive, my friend. And don't forget Fisher is the one who *threatened* to kill Asman."

"Motive," said Mrs. Roosevelt. "Motive . . . Senator Fisher and Representative Metcalf had their real or supposed motives for murdering Mr. Asman, or Preston—motives quite strong enough, whether either of them understood that Mr. Asman *was* Mr. Preston. The murder of Mr. Whatever-his-name may be wholly unrelated to the criminal activities of Shondor Jack."

"Then who murdered Shondor Jack, and why?" asked Kennelly.

Mrs. Roosevelt returned to her chair and sat down heavily. "We will know before long," she said. "When an investigation turns up more and more information, the solution to the mystery is not far off. It is only a matter of putting together the information in such a way as to lead us to the answer."

12

"The most frustrating element of criminal investigation," said Mrs. Roosevelt to Ed Kennelly and Stan Szczygiel, "is to achieve a breakthrough and then realize that your breakthrough does not solve the overall problem at all."

Szczygiel nodded. "The only thing we know tonight that we were still wondering about this morning is the meaning of the initials in the gold watch in Asman's drawer: 'JWP' was John W. Preston."

"Knowing that Asman was Preston," said the First Lady, "only adds to the frustration. Why did John Preston come to Washington and masquerade as Christian Asman? And why did two New York lawyers write letters of recommendation for a man who did not exist?"

"If I were inclined to the melodramatic," said Szczygiel, "I would wonder if Mr. Asman-Preston were not a German espionage agent."

"I have a call in to my friend Harriet Seltzer in Cleveland," said Mrs. Roosevelt. "She gave me the information about Miss Dempsey's testimony in the

Shondor Jack murder trial. Maybe she can tell me more about Mr. Preston."

"Speaking of Margaret Dempsey," said Ed Kennelly. "What have we heard from her since last night's shooting?"

"I have asked her to join us here," said Mrs. Roosevelt. "She appeared at her office about noon. She has, according to people in the West Wing, worked at her desk all afternoon—not visibly stricken."

The First Lady opened the yellow tablet on which she had been making notes. She had amended it with one strikeover:

Who might have killed Mr. Asman?

Senator Fisher (unfortunately).

~~Miss Fisher (very unlikely).~~

Congressman Metcalf (jealousy?).

Miss Dempsey (but why?).

What is connection with Miss O'Neil?

Who was "older woman" at Farragut?

Person not yet identified.

I suppose," she said, "I shall continue to think of Mr. Asman as such. But we must all make a point of thinking of him as Mr. Preston."

"I notice you have taken Joan Fisher off your list," said Kennelly. "Have we checked her story—that she was carrying bridge mix and coffee to her mother's card table?"

"We have not," said Mrs. Roosevelt. "I have another

question to ask of her. Did *she* know the true identity of Mr. Asman-Preston?"

"And what about Stormy Skye?" said Kennelly. "It seems to me a lot of people have been lying to us."

"I believe we should return to the basics," said the First Lady. "How does our new information serve to identify the murderer of the Cleveland gangster known as Shondor Jack? How does it serve to identify the murderer of Mr. Asman-Preston? Or the person who fired shots through Miss Dempsey's bathroom door?"

"I'm not sure we are any closer to answering those questions than we were before," said Szczygiel.

"Neither am I," said Mrs. Roosevelt. "And one of our chief problems is, we don't know what *motivated* the killer or killers. We have thought of several reasons why someone would have wanted to kill Mr. Asman-Preston. But we have no real idea of the motive that caused someone to kill Shondor Jack. We've got all kinds of suggestions but no firm knowledge. In the circumstances," she went on, "I think we should not put aside the possibilities that Mr. Asman-Preston was murdered by Senator Fisher, who threatened to do it, or Congressman Metcalf, who had a viable motive."

"Seems to lead us off in the wrong direction," said Kennelly.

"And let us not forget—as I wonder if we have not been too ready to do—that the two murders may not be connected at all. We have surmised that Mr. Asman-Preston killed Shondor Jack. If that is so, then someone might want revenge. But who would want revenge for the murder of Aleksandr Djaković? I am sorry to have to say this of any human being, but I have to wonder if anyone feels any remorse for that man's death. I can't help but wonder if mankind as a whole is not entitled to congratulate itself on the death of Shondor Jack."

"And on the dispatch of Asman-Preston, to be damned frank," said Kennelly. "Police work sometimes forces me to try to find and bring to punishment the killers of guys who were a curse on the world. Hell, I'd like to hang medals on some of those killers. But I can't. That's not the way the deal goes."

"Theory," said Mrs. Roosevelt. "Let us suppose that Mr. Asman-Preston, for whatever reason, left Cleveland and came here under the assumed identity of Christian Asman. Suppose Shondor Jack, who was a petty criminal, somehow identified him in Washington and threatened to reveal his duplicity. Suppose, for that reason, Mr. Asman-Preston murdered Shondor Jack. Now . . . If all those suppositions approach reality, what motive caused someone to murder Mr. Asman-Preston? Did Shondor Jack have confederates who—"

"I think it's more probable," said Kennelly, "that someone put some slugs in Asman-Preston because he was . . . Because . . . Forgive me, Mrs. Roosevelt. Because he was a cock-hound. Asman was after anything in skirts. Now that I think of it, I don't think Senator Fisher is out of the woods at all. And I don't think Congressman Metcalf is, either."

"Let us not speculate," she said. "You and Mr. Szczygiel have added a wealth of facts to our investigation today. Let us try to add some more. That's how we will reach the solution."

One possible element proved impossible for that evening. The White House operator called to say Margaret Dempsey had left a message to the effect that she was suffering a severe headache and was going home. If there were questions that absolutely had to be asked of her that evening, she could be reached at her boarding house. Otherwise she would be available in the morning.

Another element was also impossible. Harriet Seltzer was out for the evening and would return the First Lady's call tomorrow.

Mrs. Roosevelt placed a call to Joan Fisher, at home in Georgetown. The young woman was surprised by the First Lady's request to stop by for a few minutes' talk, but said she would be happy to see Mrs. Roosevelt at her convenience.

Stan Szczygiel accompanied the First Lady.

The parlor of the small brick house in Georgetown was cozy, though furnished in a somewhat heavy style. The furniture appeared to have been brought to Washington from an Arkansas farmhouse, where in a much bigger room its heaviness was not so obtrusive.

A chime clock ticked away on the mantel. Its style perhaps said more about the family than any of the other furnishings. It was made of wood polished black, and three silver-finish columns stood to each side of the clock face, each with a gilt base and cap, as though these little columns held up the lid. The clock sat on ornate gilt feet. It was a bulky thing, eighteen inches wide or more; and it sat on a small, graceful Georgian mantel above a tiny fireplace and marble hearth.

"My father and mother have gone out to dinner," said Joan Fisher. "Probably that's just as well, since I can guess what you want to talk about."

"I have just one question that I really must ask you," said Mrs. Roosevelt. "Were you aware that Christian

Asman was not Christian Asman, that he was, in fact, John Preston, a lawyer from Cleveland?"

"That explains a lot of things, doesn't it?" said Joan Fisher.

"Well . . ."

"A lot of things. It explains why he would not see Vern Metcalf. It explains why the thought of marrying me frightened him. Also why he wouldn't go places where he might be seen by a lot of people. Also why his whole life in Washington was spent at his office, at his apartment, at one or two cheap restaurants, and at the Farragut Bar."

"Did you know?" Mrs. Roosevelt asked.

Joan Fisher shook her head. "No. I had good reason to suspect, but I didn't guess."

"Do you know of any reason why he lived under an assumed name?"

"I can think of none."

Stan Szczygiel asked, "Did he have any other friends? Did you ever meet anyone else he knew?"

Joan Fisher frowned as she slowly shook her head. Then her chin snapped up, and she wagged her finger. "I didn't meet this person. But one night I went to the Farragut. Chris—or whatever his name was—had said he'd be there about nine. When I went in he was sitting with a woman. He saw me, said something to her, and she jumped up from the table and rushed into the ladies' room. Then she got out of the place somehow, so I didn't see her up close that time. I also saw her a second time. She sat at the bar looking at Chris—and at me. When I looked up and met her eye, she shoved money at the bartender and left the Farragut."

"Anyone else?"

"No."

"Well, then . . . You did *not* realize that Mr. Asman wasn't who he said he was. That is what I wanted to know. I believe we need not trouble you further, Miss Fisher."

"It has been no trouble," she said dully, and once again Mrs. Roosevelt thought she did not see enough emotion in this young woman discussing the death of a man she supposedly had hoped to marry.

As the First Lady and Stan Szczygiel stepped out onto the street, they encountered the senator and his wife, returning from what must have been an early dinner.

"As I live and breathe!" said Senator Fisher as they stood on the stoop. "My most dear lady! Whatever—"

"We stopped by to visit with Miss Fisher for a moment," said Mrs. Roosevelt. "I had some information for her about the death of Mr. Asman and hoped she might have some for me."

"Asman . . . Well, please don't leave, dear lady! You must give Mrs. Fisher and me the opportunity of extendin' our hospitality. After all, it's not often that a senator from Arkansas receives the First Lady in his home."

"Oh, Senator, we would not want to trouble you."

"Trouble? The trouble would be if we had to say we found Mrs. Franklin D. Roosevelt on our doorstoop, leavin', and couldn't persuade her to come back in for a few minutes."

It would have been most awkward to refuse. Mrs. Roosevelt introduced Stan Szczygiel, and all of them went back into the parlor. The senator sent his daughter to the kitchen for drinks, and he saw to it that the First Lady occupied what obviously was his own chair in the parlor.

Mrs. Fisher was a gray, plump woman, wearing rimless eyeglasses and looking flustered to discover herself unexpectedly hostess to Mrs. Roosevelt. She sat down on a couch and said nothing.

"Y' have new information about Asman?" the senator asked.

"Well, chiefly that he was not Asman," said the First Lady. "His name was John Preston. He was from Cleveland."

"Be damned . . . What was he doin' callin' himself Asman, then?"

"We are trying to find out."

"Uhmm . . . He was not a gentleman."

"No," agreed Mrs. Roosevelt. "He was not a gentleman."

"Y'see, Daisy?" the senator said to his wife. "I was right about Mr. Christopher Asman. He was . . . Well, what he was I can't say in terms gentlemen use before ladies."

"It is better that he is dead," said Mrs. Fisher woodenly.

"In a spirit of Christian charity, I suppose we shouldn't say that," said the senator. "In the spirit of truth, I'm glad the son of a bitch is dead."

Joan Fisher returned from the kitchen, carrying a tray covered with bottles and glasses. The senator offered bourbon and gin, with soda, nothing else. Mrs. Roosevelt tactfully accepted a shot of bourbon on ice, with a generous splash of soda.

When everyone had a drink in hand and a toast to geniality had been offered and drunk, the First Lady asked Senator Fisher, "Senator, I suppose you know that Mr. Asman-Preston was shot to death between the hours of approximately eight-thirty and nine o'clock Saturday evening. Where were you at that time?"

Senator Fisher grinned. "At the Army-Navy Club playin' poker, as I do every Saturday night," he said with an air of amused satisfaction. "At the Army-Navy Club playin' poker. Got there about a quarter after eight and didn't leave till after midnight."

"Not what Colonel Patton said," Mrs. Roosevelt remarked to Szczygiel as the agent drove her away from the house. "He said the senator didn't arrive to play poker until nine o'clock."

"One man's word against another's," said Szczygiel. "I suppose we'll have to check with the other poker players."

"I'm afraid we must," she said. "Particularly in view of the fact that Colonel Patton sincerely believes, too, that he was one of Napoleon's marshals."

"Well . . . That leaves Metcalf," said Szczygiel.

"He claims he spends his evenings at home alone, as a bachelor," said Mrs. Roosevelt. "I wonder what would happen if we dropped by his apartment unannounced?"

They'd had no dinner and so stopped at a modest restaurant and ate hamburgers. Forty-five minutes after they had left the Fisher home in Georgetown, they arrived at the ivy-covered brick apartment building that was the address of Representative Vernon Metcalf.

They entered the building and walked to the second floor, where the south front door bore Metcalf's apartment number. Stan Szczygiel rang the bell.

Representative Metcalf opened the door. "Mrs. Roosevelt! My God!"

The First Lady could see past the congressman. Over

his shoulder, she saw a young woman in a pink knit dress—that is, half out of a pink knit dress, showing all of her white underwear—scramble up from the couch and scamper toward a door.

"I am afraid we have arrived at an awkward time," said the First Lady.

Metcalf glanced behind himself and saw the young woman disappear down a hall. "Not really," he said solemnly. "It may, in fact, be very advantageous that you've come right now. I'm glad to see you, Mrs. Roosevelt."

The First Lady smiled. "Why don't you go comfort Miss Fisher and tell her she need not be embarrassed?"

The congressman led the two in. He occupied an exceptionally handsome apartment. Someone had known how to spend money, and had spent a lot of it. The living room was elegantly furnished, and either Metcalf or his decorator had known how to mix traditional pieces with contemporary ones to create a cozy, eclectic décor. Mrs. Roosevelt was not an authority on contemporary art but imagined she recognized a piece on the wall as the work of a French modernist—his name escaped her—whose paintings sold for several thousand dollars.

"Be seated, please," Metcalf said. "Let me put out something to drink."

"You needn't. We are intruding."

"Yes you are, Mrs. Roosevelt," he said frankly. "But I am glad you are. Joan came by with the information you gave her. She and I are reconciled. And if what she tells me is true, I may be able to add something to what you know about this fellow Asman, correctly known as Preston."

The First Lady and Szczygiel sat down in comfortable

overstuffed chairs upholstered in striped silk. Metcalf walked into the hall along which Joan had just fled. He stood outside a door there for a moment and spoke to her, then returned to the living room and passed through another door into what had to be the kitchen.

"'Reconciled,'" Mrs. Roosevelt said quietly to Szczygiel. "And a rescue from—"

"Arkan-sass," said Szczygiel dryly.

"Let us hope it's true."

Joan Fisher returned to the living room before the congressman. She had refastened her clothes, but her lips were swollen from fervent kissing, and her eyes were tearful.

"I told him Chris Asman was really John Preston," she whispered, "and he knew all about it. He knows all about Preston and can tell you a lot that you need to know."

"Cleveland?"

Joan Fisher nodded.

Metcalf returned from the kitchen after a minute or two, carrying a tray with bottles of brandy, Scotch, and gin. "Darling," he said to Joan, "would you mind bringing in the ice?"

He sat down and put the tray on a coffee table.

For a man who knew he was suspected of murder, Metcalf was a little too smooth for Stan Szczygiel. He wore a white shirt with the tie pulled loose. His jacket lay on a straight chair across the room.

Though she had only reluctantly drunk part of the bourbon and soda Senator Fisher had poured for her, Mrs. Roosevelt gladly accepted a splash of brandy in a snifter. What she liked about brandy was that you could sit with the snifter between your hands, sniff the liquor's delicious scent, and didn't have to be in any hurry to drink it before the ice melted.

"So . . . Asman was Preston," said the congressman. "No wonder he didn't want to see me. No wonder he refused our invitation—Joan and mine—to get together. I knew Preston in Cleveland, before he disappeared."

"Why did he disappear, Mr. Metcalf?" asked Mrs. Roosevelt.

"He was wanted by the FBI," said Metcalf. "He is—was—under indictment for stock fraud. It's a little complicated, but in essence it's the old story. He was attorney for a group that bilked people out of their money by selling them worthless stocks. It was something they all would have gotten away with before nineteen thirty-three. But it *was* a crime under the Securities Act."

"What sort of man was Mr. . . . Preston?"

Having poured drinks for the First Lady and Stan Szczygiel, then for Joan, Metcalf poured one for himself. "A smart lawyer," he said. "A good lawyer. Too smart, maybe. He defended some of the Cleveland gangsters—including, of course, Shondor Jack. God knows what they paid him. He made money. A lot of money. He did legal work for some of the bootleggers, which of course made him counsel for trucking companies after Prohibition was repealed."

"How does that make him counsel for trucking companies?" asked Szczygiel.

"If you were a beer baron with twenty-five trucks you used to haul barrels of illegal beer, and then suddenly beer was legal and the legitimate breweries started delivering again, what would you do with twenty-five trucks?" asked Metcalf. "Some of them started trucking companies."

"I have heard this before," said Mrs. Roosevelt.

"If you were a beer baron with a lot of cash on hand and no more business, you might try buying into a legitimate business and applying your old beer-baron techniques. The line between legitimate business and the rackets—which was never very well defined, to tell the truth—got very vague."

"So Mr. Preston became—"

"A lawyer who played along that line, very carefully, very successfully," said Metcalf.

"But he made a big mistake," said Joan quietly, "when he set up a phony corporation to sell phony stocks. That's what Vern was explaining to me. He was arrested. He—"

"He spent a couple of days in jail before he got himself bailed out," said Metcalf. "It must have scared the hell out of him. It wasn't a week before he disappeared. He took some money from various accounts, clients' accounts, making him an embezzler as well as a stock jobber. He was also indicted by the Cuyahoga County Grand Jury, on eight counts of embezzlement."

"Did he have a family?" asked Mrs. Roosevelt.

Congressman Metcalf nodded. "A wife. She doesn't inspire much sympathy in Cleveland. He married her for her money. She married him because—Well, Joan can explain that better than I can. The man had some kind of powerful attraction for women—though God knows why. His wife is older than he was. When he disappeared, she didn't miss a beat. I mean, she kept right on going to gallery openings, symphony concerts, country-club luncheons, meetings of the Junior League, and so on. Her family money takes good care of her."

"Children?" asked Mrs. Roosevelt.

"Yes. There's a sad story there. They had a little girl. The child is . . . How do you say it? Not quite bright. It's said of Preston in Cleveland that that kid is the only person he ever cared about."

"The child in the photograph . . ." said Mrs. Roosevelt to Szczygiel.

"Only person he ever cared about," Metcalf repeated. "Not quite so. There was a woman. Or so the story goes. Anyway, when Preston disappeared, she disappeared."

"What woman?"

"They were lovers before he married. They were lovers after. He kept her in an apartment in Rocky River. His wife knew about it and didn't care, the story is. The gossip was that his sexual demands were too great for his wife and she was glad enough to have this woman take some of the burden off her."

"Who was this woman? What *kind* of woman?"

"A nobody kind of woman," said Metcalf. "That was the point. She wasn't anybody. Preston defended her father on a bootlegging charge, and the daughter sort of came along as the fee. She was a pretty girl, and Preston set her up in a flat and kept her. She stuck with him through a marriage to another woman. They say she loves him."

"Touching story," said Joan scornfully.

"What is her name, if you know?" asked Mrs. Roosevelt.

"Beth Lasky," said Metcalf. "And one more thing about her— She is a complete, total, down-the-drain alcoholic."

"What does she look like?" asked Szczygiel.

"I never saw her," said Metcalf.

* * *

Coincidence. Lieutenant Ed Kennelly stood at the bars of the women's drunk tank, looking at a pitiful wretch of a woman who lay on the concrete floor in a stinking mess of her own vomit. The matron had used a hose to wash as much of the vomit off her as she could, but the woman had just vomited again. The matron aimed the nozzle to hose her down again, but Kennelly shook his head. The woman was shivering already.

"I jus' use a spray, Lieutenant. I don't hit 'em with a stream, except maybe once in a while when I got one screamin' her head off."

"Even so, she's cold. Lay off. I may want to question her."

He had been called because the woman had been picked up off the sidewalk in front of the Farragut Bar. The waitress, Millie, had telephoned him and said the older woman who sometimes sat with Mr. Asman had just been thrown out of the bar because she was falling-down drunk and had been taken in by the police.

"You got any identification for her?" asked Kennelly.

"Yes, sir. She's got an Ohio driver's license. It's expired, though. Says her name is Beth Lasky. It says she's thirty-one years old. Jesus! Who'd think that poor thing is just thirty-one?"

"Your name is?"

"Dixon, sir."

"Dixon, when this woman stops barfing I want you to get her out of there, get her clean, shoot her full of orange juice and coffee, and put her in a regular cell. And keep an eye on her. I don't want a suicide here. I may be wrong, but I think she may be an important witness in a big case. So you take care of her like she is somebody important. Right?"

"Right, sir."

"And whatever you do, don't let anybody bail her out. If anybody calls to ask about her, you call me. Right off! Got it?"

"Got it, sir. I'll handle it like you say." The matron frowned then. "But, Jesus, Lieutenant, can I hose her off one more time before I put her in a warm shower?"

Kennelly stood for another minute, staring at the shivering, heaving figure on the floor. His attention was focused on her hair. It was jet black.

Returning to the White House, Stan Szczygiel found waiting for him a call from Melvin Shapiro. The note said Shapiro had called, apologized for having missed Szczygiel, and promised to call again in the morning.

"I'm ready to—"

"Mr. Szczygiel," said Mrs. Roosevelt with a wry smile. "I believe you have the power of arrest. Or if you don't, Lieutenant Kennelly does. Let us make certain that Mr. Shapiro, whatever his prior commitments, appears here tomorrow afternoon at two o'clock."

"Exactly what I was about to suggest," said Szczygiel.

"Yes. Well, I have a telephone call, too. My Cleveland friend Harriet Seltzer. I believe I will return that call—after eleven though it is."

Harriet Seltzer answered her call.

"Oh, Eleanor," she said, "I was so sorry to have to leave word that I was out for the evening. I thought about it all through the dinner I attended. It occurred to me that your call was very likely important, so as soon as I got home I phoned and left a message with the White House operator."

"I am pleased that you did, Harriet," said the First Lady. "Perhaps you can confirm for me some information that has come to me from another source."

"I hope I can."

"Tell me what you know about a lawyer named John Preston."

"Oh! A horrible man! A crook! A shyster! He fled Cleveland two skips ahead of the sheriff. Disappeared. Has not been heard from since."

"What about a woman named Beth Lasky?"

"Poor child! She was Preston's mistress. The story is that she was devoted to him as no one else was. But . . . The poor young woman had very limited intellectual capacity, and besides drank too much. Came from a squalid background, you understand."

"Harriet— I have to say this in confidence at the moment. John Preston is dead. He was murdered here in Washington. I'll see that your newspaper gets the story, as soon as we can find out who killed him."

"Ah! Could have been anyone! His association with criminals . . . his aggressive frauds in stock brokering . . . Could have been anyone!"

"Harriet— What can you tell me about Congressman Vernon Metcalf?"

"Well . . . as congressmen go . . . all right. He's a product of the Cleveland political system, which doesn't recommend him. Other than that—"

"Someone has already told me he bought his seat in Congress," said Mrs. Roosevelt. "Apart from that. Personally—"

"He did do one thing here in Cleveland that was

troublesome," said Harriet Seltzer. "Oh, six or seven years ago. He was seeing a girl, and another man began to see her too. Vernon Metcalf beat that other man within an inch of his life. He was insanely jealous."

"Ah. I see. Anything more?"

"I would follow any connection with Margaret Dempsey, Eleanor. Any connection."

Ed Kennelly checked his watch. When you worked with Mrs. Roosevelt you kept strange hours. Nearly four A.M. last night. Now she had asked him to join her and Szczygiel for another of those eggs-and-coffee sessions in the White House kitchen at one A.M.

Right now, having checked and made sure that Beth Lasky was locked safely in a cell, miserable and restless but not suicidal, he had returned to the Hi-Ho Lounge.

Alphonse Tranquillo, behind his bar, immediately recognized the Irish cop and came to shove a beer on the house across the bar.

"Tell me about the broad who talked to Asman," said Kennelly. "You said a broad talked to him just before he went out the back door and got himself shot. Tell me more about her."

"Figured you'd ask," said Tranquillo. "Been lookin' for a word. Nondescript. I looked that word up in a dictionary. You know what it means, Kennelly? It means somebody that looks like anybody else, don't look like nobody special."

"But it was a broad," said Kennelly. "Blonde?"

"Naw. She was wearin' a head scarf. Most of her hair was covered, but what I see wasn't blonde. Also, she wore glasses."

"Drunk?"

"Naw. Just a broad. Nothin' special. Just a broad. You gotta understand, I wasn't lookin' close. Hell, I get a hundred like her in here in a week. She wasn't hustlin'. She wasn't drunk. She wasn't nothin' much. Only reason I noticed her at all was what you said—which is that I don't get guys like him in here every night."

"Did you ever see her before?"

Tranquillo shrugged.

Kennelly put a hand on Tranquillo's arm and closed a grip around it. "Specifically, my friend," he said. "Specifically, did this nondescript broad ever meet here with Shondor Jack?"

Tranquillo tried to pull his arm away, but Kennelly kept a hard grip on it.

"What's it to me?" Tranquillo asked.

"Nothin', I figure," said Kennelly. "So why's the question bother you?"

"It don't bother me."

"Then answer it."

Tranquillo pulled his arm away from Kennelly's now-relaxed grip. "I can't be sure," he said. "I can't say she didn't. I don't say she did, but I can't say she didn't."

"If you saw her again, you'd know her. Right? I mean, Alphonse, you remember a lot more about her now than you did when we talked about her before. I bet if we talk again you'll remember if she had blue eyes and what color lipstick she wore."

Tranquillo nodded. "You're pressurin' me. I guess I gotta say yes. If I saw her again, I'd probably know her."

"I'm goin' to arrange for you to meet her again, Alphonse," said Kennelly. "Don't plan on leavin' town or anything like that. Right?"

"Right . . . Right, Boss. I'll be here if you need me."

* * *

When Kennelly reached the White House kitchen to keep his one o'clock appointment with the First Lady, he found her and Szczygiel poring over that yellow tablet of hers. She had covered half a dozen sheets with notes. Looking at the sheets upside down, Kennelly could see dozens of question marks.

"I've got some more stuff you'll probably want to write down," he said. "You want all the details?"

"All the details, please," said Mrs. Roosevelt. "Facts, facts, facts. We've accumulated almost enough to make a solution."

"Well, to start off—" And he reported to her about the arrest of Beth Lasky and about his later conversation with Tranquillo.

She wrote notes, as he had expected.

"Tell me, Lieutenant Kennelly," she said when she had finished writing, "do you object to those confrontational meetings where various suspects and witnesses are called together and an effort is made to put all the elements of a mystery together, all at once?"

"I don't object. Not when it makes sense."

"Well, I dislike melodramatics," she said, "but I do think we may be able to solve our twin mysteries in the course of an hour or so, if we assemble the major players and make them confront each other."

"Okay," said Kennelly. "Tomorrow afternoon."

"Yes. I have appointments in the morning and a luncheon at noon, so about two tomorrow afternoon would be best for me."

"Do you think you know who killed Preston?" Kennelly asked bluntly.

"I believe I do," she said. "But I will keep my theory to myself until I see if it works out. I am going to ask you to do one more unpleasant duty in the morning. It's just possible that you may find a vital piece of evidence."

13

The President laughed at something he saw in the Thursday-morning newspapers. Missy LeHand, who had come in while he was eating from his breakfast tray and scanning his usual dozen or so papers, looked up from the *New York Herald-Tribune*, glad to see the boss had found something amusing in a generally cold assembly of news stories.

"If this continues, there'll be unemployment in the movie industry," he said, tapping the story with one finger. "It says here that Walt Disney is releasing a movie with no live actors. It will be just one great big, long cartoon. All in color, too. *Snow White and the Seven Dwarfs.* Now, that's odd. I always thought the plural of dwarf was 'dwarves.'"

"Afraid not," said Missy.

"Anyway, this movie is to be seventy-five minutes long, and not a single live actor appears in it. It will probably generate a strike."

"No doubt," she said.

"Actually, come to think of it, they'll have to use actors and actresses to do the voices; and those people will get paid and won't have to do anything but talk, like radio actors. But— An hour-and-a-quarter cartoon! I'm afraid I'd get bored."

"Did you look at this picture spread?" she asked. She picked up the *Daily News*, which had arrived on the same train that brought the *Herald-Tribune*. He had glanced at it and tossed the picture tabloid aside, but she was interested in a two-page spread of the zeppelin *Hindenburg*. "Look at those rooms! Imagine it! A luxury liner flying through the air!"

One of the photos showed passengers standing in the lounge, leaning on a rail and looking down through tilted-out windows. Another picture showed a passenger putting a pair of shoes outside his stateroom door. A steward would shine those shoes during the night, the same way it was done in a first-class hotel. Still another picture portrayed happy passengers seated around a table set with fine china and silver on heavy white linen.

The biggest picture was, of course, of the immense airship cruising over New York City. It had been taken last year, during the summer flying season—zeppelins did not cross the Atlantic in winter. The *Hindenburg* looked as if it were about to moor at the top of the Empire State Building. Prominently showing on its vertical fins were two huge swastikas, symbols of the Nazi government of Germany.

"They've announced their flight schedule for this season," said Missy.

"A little prematurely, I might tell them," said the President. "I have to give them permission to land at Lakehurst Naval Air Station. I granted permission last year, for nineteen thirty-six only. They've applied for nineteen thirty-seven, but I haven't given it yet."

"Are you thinking of not granting it?"

"Oh, not really. The company, Deutsche Zeppelin Reederei, is talking, too, about building a private airship port, just across the river from Washington. If they do that, I'm going for a ride on the *Hindenburg*. I'm reluctant to go aboard a ship bearing those big swastikas, but the adventure would be too tempting to refuse. They say they can fly from Washington to New York in well under three hours."

"I understand that Mrs. Roosevelt is having an aeronautical lunch today."

"Yes. The District of Columbia Women's Club is holding a big noon affair. With two speakers. Babs is one. Amelia Earhart is the other."

Amelia Earhart was Mrs. George Putnam. He was the famous New York publisher, and he was with her when she appeared for the annual luncheon of the D.C.W.C. The party for the head table assembled for drinks half an hour before noon. Mrs. Roosevelt accepted a sherry, as did Amelia Earhart, and the two guests of honor stood and chatted.

They had met before, more than once, when then-Governor Roosevelt and then-President Roosevelt had received A.E. as she wanted to be called, to celebrate her achievements. She had been the first woman to fly the Atlantic, then the first woman to fly the Atlantic solo, and then the first person, man or woman, to fly solo from Honolulu to California. Her exploits in the air had made her name a synonym for romantic adventure.

The aviatrix was almost as well known as the First

Lady herself. Hers was one of the most recognizable faces in the world. Her tousled hair and freckled cheeks, her solemn, penetrating eyes, and broad, friendly smile were as familiar as the features of any movie star. Her husband had an unparalleled instinct for public relations and had contributed much to keeping her name before the public.

"Well, Mrs. Putnam," said the First Lady. "Have you any additional exploits planned?"

Amelia Earhart showed Mrs. Roosevelt that disarming smile that was so much a part of her persona. "If anyone but you asked, I would not answer," she said.

"Don't feel obliged to disclose any secrets," said Mrs. Roosevelt.

A.E. grinned broadly. "Do you know how old I am, Mrs. Roosevelt?"

"I would guess—"

"Forty," said A.E. "Forty years old. How many more good flights do I have ahead of me? I've got one in mind. I'm going to try it. It caps my career, and then I'll retire." She showed the girlish smile. "Well . . . No more stunts. Just flying to get from here to there. And where I'm going is— Around the world."

"Alone?" asked Mrs. Roosevelt.

"No. I'll carry a navigator. We'll fly a Lockheed Electra. It's an extremely competent plane. The only part of the flight that is any real challenge is the Pacific. There's a tiny island out in the middle of the Pacific, called Howland Island. We've got to hit it at the end of a two-thousand-mile hop. That's the only really hard part."

"When are you leaving?"

A.E. leaned conspiratorially toward the First Lady and spoke quietly. "That's a secret. Next month. But don't tell. Around the world . . . and then peace and quiet. Okay? Peace and quiet."

Centered on the south front of the White House are three oval rooms. The most famous of these is the Blue Room, on the first floor. The oval room on the second floor, corresponding exactly to the Blue Room, was President Roosevelt's study, decorated with naval prints and ship models. The oval room on the ground floor had housed the White House boiler until, in 1902, it was rescued from that function and made a semi-formal room. President Roosevelt broadcast some of his fireside chats from it. It remained a place whose purpose was not well defined, and Mrs. Roosevelt heard no argument when she claimed it for the afternoon of Thursday, February 11, 1937.

Three tables were shoved together to make a conference table for the meeting she had called. A Stenograph reporter sat to one side, to take down whatever was said. When Mrs. Roosevelt arrived, promptly at two o'clock, the cast of characters was waiting:

—Agent Stanlislaw Szczygiel, United States Secret Service.
—Detective Lieutenant Edward Kennelly, District police.
—Senator John Fisher.
—Joan Fisher.
—Representative Vernon Metcalf.
—Margaret Dempsey, staff attorney for the Reconstruction Finance Corporation.
—Theodora "Teddy" O'Neil, call girl.

—Melvin Shapiro, New York lawyer.
—Stormy Skye, striptease dancer.
—Beth Lasky, alleged mistress of John Preston/Christian Asman.
—Alphonse Tranquillo, proprietor of the Hi-Ho Lounge.

They sat like this:

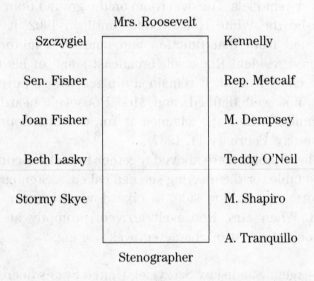

	Mrs. Roosevelt	
Szczygiel		Kennelly
Sen. Fisher		Rep. Metcalf
Joan Fisher		M. Dempsey
Beth Lasky		Teddy O'Neil
Stormy Skye		M. Shapiro
		A. Tranquillo
	Stenographer	

The First Lady could not bring herself to greet these people with a warm smile. Most of them did not want to be there. Shapiro, the New York lawyer, had protested vehemently against being forced to attend a meeting in the White House that afternoon. Senator Fisher had come only on Stan Szczygiel's assurance that his presence at the meeting would be kept confidential. Beth Lasky had been brought from jail and sat, humiliated, in a gray cotton uniform. Teddy O'Neil and Stormy Skye were apprehensive and resentful. Alphonse Tranquillo was openly afraid.

Only Representative Metcalf, Joan Fisher, and Margaret Dempsey seemed comfortable. Margaret Dempsey, who had not before smoked in Mrs. Roosevelt's presence, lit a cigarette.

"Two murders have been committed," said Mrs. Roosevelt. "First, Mr. Aleksandr Djaković, better known as Shondor Jack, was murdered in the Red Room, here in the White House, on Wednesday night of last week. Second, a man known to us as Mr. Christian Asman was murdered in the city on Saturday night. Mr. Asman, it turns out, was really a Mr. John W. Preston of Cleveland, Ohio."

She paused and looked around the room. "One of us here, at least—maybe more than one of us—knows who killed those two men, and why. Among us, we have the information to identify the murderer or murderers. I do not like dramatic confrontations, but we have experienced less than full cooperation in the investigation of these crimes. Some here have lied. When the lies are disclosed and the truth is told, we all will know who killed whom, and why."

She glanced around the table, to give every one of them a chance to disagree.

Senator Fisher cocked his head and smiled at her. Congressman Metcalf frowned grimly at the table—as did Joan Fisher. Margaret Dempsey flicked the ash of her cigarette into the glass ashtray in front of her.

"Mr. Shapiro," said the First Lady. "Why not begin with you? You wrote a letter of recommendation for Christian Asman, describing him as a fine lawyer and a Harvard classmate. In fact, no one named Christian Asman ever attended Harvard Law. What did you have in mind, Mr. Shapiro?"

Melvin Shapiro was a small, balding man, wearing round, gold-rimmed eyeglasses. He was exquisitely tailored. A yellow legal pad lay open in front of him on the table, and he had already written some notes.

"I've been turning that question over and over in my mind for some days," he said.

"And what answer have you come up with?"

"None that satisfies," he said. "In other words, I can't invent a convincing lie, though I might like to; and I can't think of anything to do but tell the truth."

"As you did not do before."

"No, as I did not do before."

"We are ready to hear the truth," said Mrs. Roosevelt.

Shapiro took a moment to light a cigar. It would help him calm his nerves, apparently. For a moment the ritual of holding flame to cigar and drawing in smoke seemed to hold his entire attention; then he began to talk:

"John Preston . . . We called him Jack. Jack Preston. We *were* at Harvard together. Not in the same class—I was a year ahead of him—but we were there at the same time and knew each other. We were friends."

"And was Mr. Jonathan Merrill his friend, too?" asked the First Lady.

"Sure. Johnny. Johnny Merrill. We couldn't have two Johns or Johnnies, so we called Preston Jack. Right. We were friends. I don't mean to say we were each other's very closest, most devoted friends, but we certainly knew and liked each other. So . . . When John Preston graduated, he went home to Cleveland. It was his home town. I told him he ought to practice law in New York, which was where the real money and prestige were, but he wanted to do it in Cleveland. So Cleveland it was. And I didn't see him any more. I heard from him once a year, saw him once every two years, when he came to New York. Always enjoyed his company."

"Did you know what happened to him in Cleveland, that he was indicted for stock fraud?"

Shapiro smiled wryly and put his cigar aside. "He was indicted, Mrs. Roosevelt, under the Securities Act of 1933. That law was—and is—a piece of social experimentation enacted (you will forgive me) with your husband's backing to impose some professorish theories on the nation's money markets. The Securities Act outlaws perfectly sound, ordinary, and traditional business practices that have existed for decades . . . no centuries. What was smart, shrewd business in nineteen thirty-two became a crime in nineteen thirty-three—and, I firmly believe, will no longer be a crime after, let us say nineteen forty-one."

"What you call 'sound, ordinary, and traditional business practices' includes insider trading, pools, wash sales, lists of preferred buyers, and so on," said Mrs. Roosevelt coldly. "It includes deception, as its basis, does it not? 'The fool and his money are soon parted.' Hmm?"

"Without meaning to argue with you, Mrs. Roosevelt," said Shapiro, "are you familiar with the terms *malum in se* and *malum prohibitum*?"

"I believe so. But you define them, Mr. Shapiro."

"An act *malum in se*," he said, "is an act like murder, kidnapping, rape, arson, et cetera, that is wrong *per se*, whether a legislative body calls it wrong or not. An act *malum prohibitum* is an act that is not inherently wrong but is a crime only because some legislative body says it is. The law that Jack Preston violated prohibits things that are not morally or inherently wrong but have been defined as crimes by a single Congress. Another Congress may repeal those prohibitions. Frankly, Johnny Merrill and I regarded Jack Preston as a victim: the victim of your husband's professors and social theorists."

"So you helped him to create a false identity," she said.

"That's right. We didn't think he'd done anything wrong. Anyway he was a fellow Harvardian, and a man owes something to that."

"Yes," she said crisply. "My husband graduated from Harvard College."

"Why, in the name of God," asked Kennelly, "did a guy with his kind of ideas and feelings want to work in the White House? Of all places? Why would you send Preston a recommendation to work in the Roosevelt administration?"

"Well . . . They were looking for him," said Shapiro. "It was his idea to hide here. It seemed like the cleverest thing in the world. Wanted by the FBI, and working in the Executive Wing of the White House!"

"Did you know he was wanted for embezzlement as well as for violations of the securities laws?" asked Mrs. Roosevelt.

Shapiro frowned and put his cigar aside. "No," he said.

She stared at him for a moment. "Embezzlement is *malum in se*, is it not?"

Shapiro nodded glumly.

"But there are others here who knew that 'Mr. Asman' was in reality Mr. Preston." She glanced around the table. "Are there not?"

Margaret Dempsey crushed her cigarette. "Yes. I knew."

"You knew Mr. Preston rather well, didn't you, Miss Dempsey? Mr. Preston defended Mr. Djaković—Shondor Jack—against a charge of murder in the first degree, and you were the star witness for the defense."

Margaret Dempsey nodded. "When I first saw him here in the White House, in the Executive Wing, I thought I'd seen a ghost. I'd had word from Cleveland, from my father, that Preston had probably been murdered. But here he was! Well, he took me aside and explained what he was doing. I didn't know what to do. I felt sorry for him. And, after all, I'm a Harvardian myself. So I kept my mouth shut, and I suppose I shouldn't have."

"But you had reason to, didn't you?" said Mrs. Roosevelt. "Let us say a good many thousands of reasons, on deposit in a Pittsburgh bank."

Margaret Dempsey's face flushed shining pink, and her jaw set tight.

Mrs. Roosevelt nodded. "Who killed Shondor Jack? Miss Lasky, I suspect you know."

Beth Lasky ran her hands down over her shabby, ill-fitting gray jail uniform. "Maybe I do," she said. "And maybe I don't."

"But you'd like to know who killed Mr. Preston, wouldn't you?"

The woman ran her eyes around the table, looking at everyone. "All of 'em had somethin' to do with it," she said.

Beth Lasky was a plump, bright-eyed woman with a ravaged complexion. The corners of her mouth turned down and ended in two wrinkles that descended toward her jawline. She nodded emphatically and did not repeat what she had said: that all of them had something to do with the death of Preston.

"Not me," said Stormy Skye. "I had nothin' to do with it."

"You slept with him," said Beth Lasky sullenly.

"Twice. Just twice. And the night he was killed, I was dancin' in my birthday suit. I had nothin' to do with his gettin' killed."

"Where do you live, Miss Lasky?" asked the First Lady.

"I got a room."

"You spent a lot of nights with Preston," said Kennelly.

She shrugged. "Yeah. For the last ten years. But it was always somethin'. Always somebody else. And always a reason. Always had to see another girl . . . somebody, 'cause she could do somethin' good for him. I couldn't just move in with him here in Washington, 'cause that would spoil his chances of latchin' onto somethin' good. Besides, I wasn't supposed to be seen with him. Somebody might see me with him and figure it out. When I went to see him, I had to sneak up to his place late at night."

"He wasn't a very nice man," said Margaret Dempsey.

"Best *I* had," said Beth Lasky, and she covered her face with her hands and sobbed.

"Senator Fisher," said Mrs. Roosevelt. "You said you arrived at the Army-Navy Club at eight-fifteen on Saturday night. You didn't. Why did you say you did?"

Senator Fisher lifted his chin high. "I was . . . Hell, I can prove where I was."

"If so, why did you tell us you were at the Army-Navy Club forty-five minutes before you got there?"

"Because I didn't want to say where I was the hour

before. But I can prove where I was, easy enough, if I have to."

"Let's say you have to, Senator," said Kennelly.

The senator looked at Stormy Skye and smiled lazily. "Somethin' unusual happened durin' your act, first show Saturday night. Don't tell 'em what it was. *I'll* tell em. Then you tell 'em if I'm right."

She frowned at him but nodded her head.

"You fell down," he said. "Damn near fell off the stage."

"A heel broke, on one of my shoes," said Stormy Skye.

Joan Fisher laughed nervously.

"Congressman Metcalf?" asked Mrs. Roosevelt.

"I've got nothing to add to what I told you before," said the congressman. "I was at home alone. For all I can prove, I could have gone out and killed Preston. I still thought he was Asman and didn't know who he was or what he looked like, but I've got no witness to prove I didn't do it."

The First Lady turned to Ed Kennelly and smiled. "Well," she said. "I suppose we had better make our case, Lieutenant."

Kennelly nodded.

"Mr. Tranquillo," said Mrs. Roosevelt. "You say Mr. Preston spoke briefly with a woman before he left your lounge on Saturday evening. Is that young woman here?"

Alphonse Tranquillo had not been able to conceal his acute discomfort at being in this place. Now he blushed and stuttered. "I . . . I can't say . . . not for sure. "I . . . I just ain't sure." He glanced at Teddy O'Neil. "She could might be." He glanced at Margaret Dempsey. "*She* might could be. I don't think the blonde young lady. And it wasn't Stormy there. She's too tall."

"You said the young woman was wearing a scarf over her hair," said Mrs. Roosevelt.

"Yes, and a pair of glasses."

The First Lady reached into a paper bag beside her chair. "Was it perhaps this scarf?" she asked, pushing a red and white head scarf across the table.

Tranquillo nodded. "Yeah. Could be. Sure, it could be. Red and white like that. That kind of little pattern. Yeah. That—"

"If one of these young women put it around her head, would that help you to recognize her?"

"Yeah . . ."

"And eyeglasses," said Mrs. Roosevelt. She reached down again and pulled from the bag a pair of spectacles. "Odd glasses," she said. "Not lenses. Just glass. Would you accommodate us by trying on the scarf and glasses, Miss Dempsey?"

"No, I won't," said Margaret Dempsey sharply.

"Well, it makes little difference," said the First Lady. "Since the scarf and fake spectacles came from your room, we know they are yours. And I think the rest of it fits together."

"From *my* room?"

"I asked Lieutenant Kennelly to enter your room again this morning and search for the scarf and eyeglasses. I'm afraid you are guilty of murder, Miss Dempsey. I'm afraid also you are guilty of hubris. If you had been a little less confident of yourself and had disposed of the scarf and eyeglasses, it might have been a good deal more difficult to make a case against you—though I think we could have done it. You tipped yourself when you fired five pistol shots through your own bathroom door. In my mind, you have been the chief suspect in the murder of Mr. Asman-Preston since that night."

Kennelly put handcuffs on Margaret Dempsey. "You are charged with the murder of one John W. Preston, otherwise known as Christian Asman. It may go better with you if you tell the truth. I can't promise anything of that kind, but it may go better for you."

She sat and for two whole minutes stared at the handcuffs on her wrists, stared without showing a sign of a tear. She breathed deeply, but otherwise she showed no emotion.

Then she looked at Mrs. Roosevelt. "What do you want to know?" she asked.

The First Lady sighed. "To start with, Shondor Jack paid you ten thousand dollars to testify falsely at his murder trial in nineteen-thirty. Is that not true?"

Margaret Dempsey nodded.

"You gave him the alibi that allowed him to escape conviction on a charge of which he was guilty."

"Yes."

"No one knew," Mrs. Roosevelt went on. "Not even your father . . . No one but Shondor Jack and John Preston."

Margaret Dempsey nodded. "My father is an honorable lawyer. He detested a man like Preston. Anyway . . . Shondor Jack could have used any of a dozen girls for his witness, but it was a whole lot more clever—and a whole lot more effective—to use me. Preston contacted me and made the offer. I accepted it."

"It was suspected in Cleveland," said the First Lady. "So when you yourself became a lawyer, you couldn't practice there."

"I could have. But not in a good firm, the way my father wanted me to."

"So you entered government service," said Mrs. Roosevelt. "And you did well, too."

"I am a good lawyer," said Margaret Dempsey.

"Well . . . I am not so sure. Anyway, when did you encounter Mr. Preston here in Washington?"

"As soon as he got here. Not long after. He wanted me to sleep with him. I made it very clear to him that nothing of the kind was going to happen. He made quite an appeal, suggested we were old friends, and so on; but I would not sleep with him. To tell the truth, I didn't like him. I never did."

"Miss Lasky," said Mrs. Roosevelt. "When did you arrive in Washington?"

"I got here before he did. He gave me some money and told me to come to Washington and rent myself a room. I was supposed to send a postcard to a lawyer in New York. Not this one here, the other one: Merrill. Just write my address on the postcard, nothin' else. He showed up in a couple weeks. He stayed with me in that room till he got his job and his apartment. Those were good weeks."

"Does anyone know how long it was before Mr. Preston, in the guise of Asman, met Shondor Jack?" the First Lady asked.

"I can tell you," said Teddy O'Neil. She paused to light a Wings. "Like I said last time I talked with Kennelly, I haven't been back to Cleveland in a long, long time. But I have friends there. I keep in touch, a little. Friends . . . They told Shondor where I was. They told Preston. When those guys came to Washington, both of them looked me up. I'm not hard to find. What I do is a sort of a public kind of business. Bartenders, cabbies, guys like that, know about the redhead. There aren't too many of us in Washington, not redheads anyway. So anyway, Shondor found me and put his hooks in me again. Then when Preston showed up, he found me, too."

"You were working for Shondor Jack at that point," said Kennelly.

"Yeah. Well . . . mostly. He didn't know everything. Anyway, Preston found me. He wanted a . . . relationship. We went to his apartment. He paid me, but he said he couldn't afford that kind of money, and he wanted me free. I said no. But he kept after me and kept after me. He'd call me. A couple of times Shondor answered the phone, but he didn't know who was on the line. Then Preston started seeing me at the Farragut Bar and giving me a rush. I told him to leave me alone. Finally I told Shondor about him."

"How did Shondor Jack react to that?" asked Mrs. Roosevelt.

"The guy couldn't have been happier," said Teddy O'Neil. "He couldn't stop laughing."

"Why?"

"He figured he'd get some money out of Preston."

"Blackmail."

Teddy O'Neil dragged on her cigarette. "I guess that's what it's called," she said.

Margaret Dempsey was trying to light a cigarette but, in handcuffs, found it awkward. Metcalf struck a match for her.

"Long as I'm supposed to get something out of being honest, I'll pick the story up from here," she said. "Shondor showed up at the White House. He sent word to Preston—calling him Asman, of course—that he wanted an appointment. He used the name Aleksandr

Djaković. He came to put a squeeze on Preston. But . . . In the hall. On the second floor in the Executive Wing . . . The son of a bitch ran into me!"

Margaret Dempsey turned and spoke to Teddy O'Neil. "You think finding out Preston was in town made Shondor happy? You have no idea how happy it made him to see me. He told me I had to meet him for dinner. And over that dinner he told me he wanted his ten thousand dollars back."

"Did you refuse?" asked Mrs. Roosevelt.

"Yes. So he threatened to reveal the whole thing. He couldn't be tried again on the murder. He'd been acquitted. But I could be tried for perjury. I could be disbarred. Shondor Jack wouldn't even have had to appear. Or so he said. And I was in a panic and didn't really think it through."

"But you didn't kill Shondor Jack," said Mrs. Roosevelt.

"No. John Preston killed him. But I was in the hall outside. I had a pistol in my purse, and I was our second line of defense. If Shondor had gotten away from Preston, I planned to follow him out on the White House grounds, in the dark, and shoot him."

"Shondor Jack had separated himself from a tour group that morning," said Stan Szczygiel. "He had unlatched a ground-floor window so he could get back in that night. Also, he'd stolen a telephone list. As soon as he got inside the White House, he telephoned Preston and demanded Preston come and meet him."

"It was Shondor who said Red Room," Margaret Dempsey continued. "He'd taken the tour of the White House several times and knew his way around. I don't know why he picked the Red Room or how he got there."

"My theory is he came up the east stairs," said Szczygiel. "That's farthest from the State Dining Room and the people serving. I figure he ducked across the hall and into the Green Room. Then he just went through the Green Room and Blue Room and into the Red Room."

"He wanted to show Preston, and maybe me, that he could go wherever he wanted," said Margaret Dempsey. "Anyway, Preston and I had talked about solving our problem by killing Shondor. And Preston decided he would do it, right then, if he could. Finding the body in the White House would confuse the investigation, he said."

"Where did he get the knife?" asked Kennelly.

"I don't know."

"Where did you get the pistol?"

"I'd had it a long time. A *long* time."

"Why'd you have to kill John?" Beth Lasky sobbed.

Margaret Dempsey raised her chin high, defiantly. "After he killed Shondor Jack, he told me *he* wanted my ten thousand dollars. Said he needed it more than I did. He—"

"How in the world did he know you hadn't spent it?" asked Mrs. Roosevelt.

"He'd deposited it in my name in the bank in Pittsburgh. He and Shondor had some way of knowing I hadn't withdrawn it. I guess they'd paid off a bank clerk—or something like that."

Everyone kept silent for a moment, as if all of them needed time to absorb what they had heard.

Margaret Dempsey allowed them only moments before she continued. "I'd rather have given him the money than kill him," she said. "But I knew that wouldn't be the end of it. All my life, whenever he thought he needed money, he'd have come to me and told me he needed whatever I had—needed it worse than I did. That was the kind of man he was. He couldn't go back to a lucrative practice. Sooner or later he'd have been on the lam again. He'd have blackmailed me for the rest of my life."

"You met him at the Hi-Ho Lounge," said Kennelly.

"His idea. But I went there a couple of hours before and checked the place out. Then I didn't keep my appointment with him. I was late. He sat and drank while he waited, the way I figured he would. I wore the scarf and fake glasses. But he knew me. I was supposed to hand over the pass book to the Pittsburgh account. I told him I wouldn't do it there in the bar; he'd have to come out back, to a private place. He was so drunk that seemed logical to him. So he went out in the alley with me."

"Why'd you blow holes in your bathroom?" asked Kennelly with a wry smile.

"'Cause I'm strictly an amateur at this kind of thing and thought I could divert attention from myself by making it look like somebody'd tried to kill me, too."

"One more thing," said Mrs. Roosevelt. "You committed a burglary too, didn't you?"

Margaret Dempsey shrugged. "What difference does that make now? Yes. I did."

"You took two things. A photograph of a child and a gold watch."

"No one knew he was Preston yet. The longer everybody thought he was Asman, the better for me. It's just possible you might have buried him and never figured out Christian Asman was John Preston."

"Where are the watch and the picture?"

"In the Potomac, along with the pistol. If anyone had searched my room that night when the doctor gave me a sedative, they'd have found the pistol under the mattress. I was lying on it. I tried not to go to sleep while anyone was still in the room with me. But the sedative worked, and I slept all night on that revolver."

EPILOGUE

Mrs. Roosevelt was surprised at the amount of sympathy Margaret Dempsey received. The First Lady was herself sympathetic on a personal basis, but she was surprised to learn that a great many people seemed to hold the opinion that all Margaret Dempsey had done was kill a blackmailer who was under indictment for other serious crimes and that maybe she had not served society so ill after all.

Margaret was represented by a competent attorney. In May he arranged for her to plead guilty to a charge of murder in the second degree. She was sentenced to serve ten to twenty years in prison.

In 1939, Margaret Dempsey, then confined in the federal prison for women in West Virginia, was the subject of a series of feature articles in the Cleveland *Press.* They were sympathetic and suggested she should be pardoned before she served out her ten-year minimum. Later, she was the subject of articles in other newspapers and two magazines. They, too, were sympathetic. Margaret Dempsey became something of a celebrity.

A formal application for pardon was made in 1943. Burdened with wartime responsibilities, the President hardly took note of it. He asked Mrs. Roosevelt for a suggestion or recommendation, and Mrs. Roosevelt said she had none to offer, either way.

In January 1946, Mrs. Roosevelt was in London for the first meeting of the United Nations General Assembly. A reporter stopped her in the lobby of her hotel and asked her if she thought Margaret Dempsey should be pardoned. Mrs. Roosevelt said she had no opinion. Passed on by the reporter's wire service, "no opinion" became "no objection." On January 28, 1946, President Harry Truman signed, not a pardon, but a commutation of sentence to time already served. Margaret Dempsey was released.

She returned to Cleveland, where she lived with her parents on a suburban estate. Her mother died in 1947, her father in 1948. With her inheritance, Margaret Dempsey bought a waterfront villa at Palm Beach. She never married. She became an art collector and a breeder of toy dogs. It was remarked of her in her later years that she was quite eccentric and apparently rather lonely, though she was always surrounded by half a dozen yapping little dogs. She died in 1989, at the age of seventy-nine.

Joan Fisher married Vernon Metcalf. He was elected to five more terms in Congress, then was appointed a federal judge by President Truman. President Lyndon Johnson appointed him to the United States Circuit Court of Appeals. The Metcalfs had three sons. The judge retired in 1976.

Melvin Shapiro and Jonathan Merrill were formally reprimanded by the Association of the Bar of the City of New York for their part in the Preston-Asman deception.

Teddy O'Neil continued as a high-priced call girl until 1946, when she retired. She married one of her former clients, an Under-secretary of the Interior and moved with him to Colorado when the Eisenhower Administration replaced her husband with a Republican. She and her husband lived on a ranch. They had a son and a daughter.

Stormy Skye took pity on Beth Lasky and got her a job as wardrobe mistress for her travelling troupe of strip-teasers. A year later Beth married one of the baggy-pants comics in the show. He urged Beth to supplement their income by stripping on stage, and for a couple of years she did, always as a very minor performer. When Beth gave up the stage, she became a ticket taker at the Gayety and continued there as long as the theater remained open.

Stan Szczygiel retired in 1939 at age 65. He moved to Florida and began to invest in real estate, at first modestly, then on a much larger scale. When he died in 1961, his estate was valued at $14 million.

Ed Kennelly remained with the D.C. police department. He rose to the rank of captain and chief of detectives. He and Mrs. Roosevelt cooperated on several other investigations.

Amelia Earhart never returned from the round-the-world flight she described to Mrs. Roosevelt.